Fruit and Nutcase

JEAN URE

Illustrated by Mick Brownfield

First published in Great Britain by Collins 1998
First published in paperback by Collins 1999
This edition published by HarperCollins *Children's Books* 2001
HarperCollins *Children's Books* is a division of HarperCollins*Publishers* Ltd
77–85 Fulham Palace Road, Hammersmith, London W6 8JB

The HarperCollins website address is
www.harpercollins.co.uk

8

Text copyright © Jean Ure 1998
Illustrations copyright © Mick Brownfield 1998

ISBN-13   978 0 00 712153 3

Mixed Sources
Product group from well-managed
forests and other controlled sources
www.fsc.org Cert no. SW-COC-1806
© 1996 Forest Stewardship Council

FSC is a non-profit international organisation established to promote the
responsible management of the world's forests. Products carrying the FSC
label are independently certified to assure consumers that they come
from forests that are managed to meet the social, economic and
ecological needs of present and future generations.

Find out more about HarperCollins and the environment at
www.harpercollins.co.uk/green

For my very own Fruit & Nut Case...
and for Sydenham High School who gave me
such a warm welcome

Chapter One

My dad's an Elvis Presley look-alike. He's got a white suit just like Elvis had, and a guitar, and he sings all the songs that Elvis sang. *Blue Suede Shoes*, *Hound Dog*, *Love me Tender, Love me True*. He knows them all!

I've drawn a picture of my dad being Elvis on my bedroom wall. I'll
draw it again, now.

I'm always
drawing on my
bedroom wall.
When I've filled
up all the space
I'm going to
start on the
ceiling. I'll be
taller by then. I'll
stand on a stepladder
and I'll be able to reach.

This is how one bit of my bedroom wall looks.

It's instead of having a garden. As a matter of fact there is a garden at the back of this house, but it belongs to old Misery Guts that lives downstairs and she won't let me play in it. It's only a bit of moth-eaten grass and dustbins, anyhow. If I had a garden I would grow all flowers in it.

My *garden* wall is right opposite my bed where I can see it when I wake up in the morning. My *people* wall is by the windows.

Unfortunately, that is all the wall there is as the room is not very big and there is a huge great enormous old-fashioned wardrobe just inside the door, taking up loads of valuable space.

The wardrobe used to belong to my nan. I hate it! When I was little, like four or five, I used to think fierce monsters lived in it. I don't now, of course; now that I'm older. But I still hate it because it is *ugly*. I hate things that are ugly!

Dad is always promising that he will chop it up and make me a shelf out of it, but so far he hasn't. He's better at being Elvis than at D.I.Y.

Sometimes, like if we're having a bit of a party, Dad will put on his Elvis suit and sing *Love me Tender* specially for Mum. *Love me Tender* is her favourite. She goes really gooey over that one!

In case there is anybody who has just dropped by from another planet and is thinking "Who is this Elvis person?" I maybe ought to explain that Elvis Presley was a very famous singer way back in my nan's time. Mum says he was called Elvis-the-Pelvis because he used to wiggle his hips around as he sang, but Dad says he was the King of Rock, and that is what some people still call him, "the King".

My dad is a dead ringer for the King! He looks really great when he brushes his hair back and puts gel on it so that it puffs up in front, the way the King's did. And he wears his white suit and his high-heeled boots and he sings all these old songs. OK, and Mum loves it.

They get all moony and swoony the pair of them. It's like they're teenagers again, before I was born.

Once upon a time, Dad used to do Elvis gigs in the local clubs but he hasn't done one for a while now. Last time he did one he had a bit of an accident. He tripped over his guitar lead and fell off the stage and busted his ankle.

🐱 astrophe!

Dad's always doing things to himself.

He's a real disaster area!

My mum's not much better. She does the daftest things!

Honestly, my parents! They're going to turn me into a right fruit and nut case, I know they are.

I try to look after them, but I can't have my eye on them all of the time.

Dad gets ever so impatient when Mum messes up the dinner or burns his shirts. But she can't help it! It's just the way she is.

Like Dad flying off the handle. He can't help it, either; he's just a live wire. He doesn't mean anything by it. But it gets Mum all flustered and nervous and I have to go jumping in really fast and make them laugh. I can always make them laugh! Usually.

When we're having fun together, like when Dad's being Elvis singing his songs, and Mum's dancing along to them, life's absolutely brilliant. I think they're the best mum and dad in the world and I don't care a row of pins that we haven't any money and have to live in the upstairs part of a rotten crumbly old house with Misery Guts lurking like some horrible evil spider waiting to catch us in her web. It just doesn't bother me in the slightest little bit. It doesn't bother me *where* I live so long as I'm with my mum and dad.

It's when Mum does something daft and Dad flies off the handle and makes her cry that I get a bit fussed. What scares me is in case they stop loving each other and Dad goes off to live somewhere else, so that we're not a family any more. That is the ONLY THING in the universe that I am scared of. I'm not scared of climbing trees right to the very top, I'm not scared of big fierce dogs that run barking at you, I'm not scared of Tracey Bigg and her gang of stupid bullies, no way! I could bash Tracey Bigg to a pulp any time I want. But I don't think I could bear it if my mum and dad split up.

Every night before I go to sleep I say this special prayer. I haven't ever let on to anyone about my prayer before, not a single living soul, but Cat told me I'd got to be honest.

Cat's the one who said I ought to write a book. She said, "I just know that you can do it, Mandy!" I said, "You mean, like… a book about *me*?" and Cat said, "Well, and why not?" So then I didn't know what I would have to write about, or what sort of things she'd want me to put, and she said, "It'll be a true story, right? *Your* story. So just tell it like it really is."

All this stuff about myself. I dunno! It seems weird. But if it's what Cat wants.

So, all right! I'm being honest. I AM BEING HONEST! Watch my lips.

I don't know – *honestly* – whether I really believe in God, but that doesn't stop me saying my prayer. This is what I pray:

Actually, I don't do that. Kneel, I mean. I sort of put my hands together, but I do it under the duvet when I'm lying in bed. I've been doing it for almost two years, now.

Two years is a long time to keep on saying the same prayer. But it's worked, so far! Even if Dad does sometimes fly off the handle. Even if Mum does do the daftest things. We're still all together! I wouldn't ever dream of going to sleep without saying my prayer.

"Please, God, don't let Mum and Dad get divorced. Please, God! Let them be together for ever and ever, and ever and ever, and ever and ever, and ever and ever, and ever and ever, amen."

I have to say it ten times, to match my age. The older I get, the more difficult it will be to keep count of all the for evers! But I will still do it. I will always do it.

My life is quite uneventful, really, and I cannot think there is going to be very much to record, but Cat says, "Go for it! Just put whatever occurs to you. Whatever's important."

But now that I've said about my prayer, and about Mum and Dad, I can't think of anything else! Just being together as a family is all that is important.

Maybe I should describe "A Day in the Life of Mandy Small". It is not what I would call very interesting, but I expect Cat would like it.

OK. Well. I always set my special Mickey Mouse alarm clock so's to be sure of waking up on time in the morning. As soon as it rings I leap madly out of bed and hurriedly rush into my clothes.

If it's summer I do it more slowly, but in the winter I have to rush or I would freeze to an icicle before I got through dressing. This is because we don't have any central heating in this crumbly old house. Sometimes it is so cold that when I wake up there are frost patterns on my window, all swirly and beautiful.

Once I am into my clothes I go racing to Mum's room to make sure that she is awake. Dad has to leave home at six o'clock to go and clean windows with his friend Garry, and sometimes after he's gone Mum falls asleep again. If I don't wake her she would be late for work and then she would be threatened with the sack, which is what happened once before.

My nan says, "Oh, really, Sandra!" (Sandra is my mum's name.) "Fancy having to rely on a child to get you up! Why on earth don't you set your alarm?"

But the one time Mum set the alarm for seven, after Dad had gone off, she forgot to put it back again to 5.30 and Dad didn't wake up next morning, so then *he* was late and that made him fly off the handle, and that is why I have taken charge. It is easier for me to do it. I don't mind waking up.

After I have shaken Mum, I go into the kitchen and make some tea and toast. I then go back to Mum's room to check that she is still awake. Sometimes she is, but more often she has gone and nodded off again. It isn't Mum's fault that she can't wake up in the mornings. She's just not very good at it. Some people are and some people aren't, and Mum is one of the ones that aren't. But it's all right, because she's got me. She says, "What I'd do without my Mand, I don't know."

Mum is Sand and I am Mand. I think that's really neat!

Dad is Barry. It occurs to me that if they had another baby and it was a boy, they could call it Harry and then we would have Barry and Harry, and that would be neat, as well. I'd quite like a baby brother, but Nan says, "Heaven forbid! They can't even cope with one of you." So I don't think, alas, that they will have another baby. Apart from anything else, where would it sleep?

All we have in this upstairs part of the house is one bedroom for Mum and Dad, one (*tiny* little) bedroom for me, one room for sitting in, one which is a kitchen, and one which is the bathroom, though that is just a measly bit of room shaped like a wedge of cheese, half-way down the stairs, that we have to share with old Misery Guts, who moans like crazy about tide marks round the bath and hairs in the wash basin. She also used to moan about us using her loo paper, so now she carries her own roll with her whenever she goes there.

Now I've forgotten where I was.

I know! Telling about my day.

So. Right. As soon as I've eaten a bit of toast, and Mum's had her cup of tea, we go down the stairs, on tiptoe because of Misery Guts, and close the front door behind us *really quietly*, and run up the road together, laughing, as it is always a relief to know that a) Mum is not late and won't be threatened with the sack and b) we have not disturbed old Misery Guts and been yelled at.

Poor Mum! She hates being yelled at. She's quite a timid person, really. I am more like Dad. I am FIERCE. What my nan calls "aggressive and up-front". But she can talk! We both take after her. Dad's dad, my grandy, is well under her thumb. That's what Mum says, anyway.

Mum hasn't got a mum and dad. She was dumped when she was just a little kid. I think it must be so terrible to feel that you're not wanted. That is something I have *never* felt. I know I was a mistake, because Nan has often told me so. She says that Mum and Dad were "no more than children themselves" and "far too young to go having babies". But once they'd got over their surprise they were really pleased. Mum says I'm the cleverest thing she's ever done. She says, "Your dad was so excited! He even came to the hospital to see you arrive!"

So I know that I am loved and wanted. I just wish I could be certain that Mum and Dad love and want each other. I think they do, 'cos they always kiss and make up and Dad is always buying Mum little presents to show how much she means to him. But it just would be nice to be certain *sure*.

Now I've gone and lost track again. Miss Foster – she's our teacher at school – she'd say I'm not concentrating. She's always accusing me of not concentrating.

OK. So now I am! This is what happens after me and Mum have left the house.

We walk as far as the tube station together, then Mum kisses me goodbye and I go on to school. I always turn at the corner and wave, and

Mum waves back. For the rest of the day, I can't wait for school to end so that I can go back home again.

I can't stand school. There's this girl in my class called Tracey Bigg who really bugs me. She's really got it in for me. This is because one time when Oliver Pratt was blubbing and Tracey Bigg and her mates were making fun of him, I went to his rescue. Like Tracey was jeering at him and calling him a crybaby so I told her to stop it and she said, "Who do you think you are?" and I said I knew who I was and if she didn't shut her mouth I'd shut it for her and she goes, "Oh, yeah?" and I go, "Yeah," and we have this huge big fight and Oliver just stands there with his finger in his mouth, gorming. I mean, he is a total nerd but he can't help it. I don't expect he can. It isn't any reason to be horrid to him. But lots of people are, like Billy Murdo and his gang. *Bully* Murdo, I call him.

See, if you're not the same as all the rest, you get picked on. Oliver's not the same 'cos he's a bit, well, sort of slow; and I'm not the same 'cos – I don't really know why I'm not the same. But Miss Foster's always getting at me and making me feel like I'm useless. I wish I could go to an acting school! One of those places where sometimes the kids get picked to be on telly. I bet I'd be good at that! But probably, I expect, you need lots of money, like you do for most things. So until some big pot film person catches sight of me and goes "Hey! Wow!" and instantly offers me a Lead Part in his next production, it looks like I am *stuck*. Worse luck.

The minute school is over I go scooting off just as fast as I can to collect Mum from her baker's shop, where she works, and we go round the supermarket together and buy stuff for tea and carry it home and hope old Misery isn't waiting to pounce on us the minute the front door opens, which all too often she is.

After we've listened politely to old Misery and meekly promised to mend our ways, we go upstairs and have a cup of something and a giggle before getting the tea ready for Dad. Me and Mum do a lot of giggling. We're like sisters, sometimes, the two of us.

Dad comes in at five o'clock and I always go rushing to meet him. Sometimes, if old Misery's caught him, he'll be in a right grumpy mood. And when Dad's in a grumpy mood, BEWARE! Mum gets flustered, and that's when things start to go wrong – specially if she's done something daft and ruined his tea.

But if he's in a good mood, then whoopee! We have fun. Maybe he'll sing some Elvis, or we'll play a game of cards, or just settle down to watch the telly like any other family. If it's summer I might perhaps go into my room to do some more wall-painting. I aim to get the walls filled up by the time I'm eleven! Then it's the ceiling. After that, who knows? The floor???

Nan thinks it's terrible I'm allowed to paint on the walls, but Dad says it's my room, so why shouldn't I? He says, "Other kids get to play with their computers: Mandy gets to paint her bedroom."

That is one of the very *best* things about my dad. He always, always sticks up for me!

I'm not really actually writing this. I am saying it into a tape machine!

It was Cat's idea. Cat is the person who comes into school every week to help people like me and Oliver with our reading. She is my friend. And it's all right for me to call her Cat and not Miss Daley; she said that I could. She didn't say that Oliver could. Just me. Because we're friends.

Cat knows I'm not very good at writing. But I'm ace at talking! Usually. It all depends who I'm with; I don't just talk to anyone. My nan complains I never stop but that's not true. Sometimes I don't say a word for minutes on end. And when I'm at school I don't hardly talk at all, except just sometimes to Oliver, 'cos of feeling sorry for him. If I didn't talk to him, nobody would. So we talk about a few things, but nothing important.

Cat is the only person I **really** talk to. I can talk about anything to Cat! What I usually do, I tell her the latest joke I've heard or something funny about old Misery Guts and we have a bit of a laugh. I don't tell her about hating school or Miss Foster having a go at me or anything like that. That would be whingeing and I hate people that whinge. But I *could* tell her. If I wanted. And I know that she'd listen 'cos she's that sort of person. She's not just my friend, she's my *special* friend; and that's why I'm doing this book. Because she asked me.

When I've filled up the tape, or done as much as I can, Cat's mum is going to type it out on her word processor and then Cat is going to get it printed. It will all be spelt right, with lots of commas and full stops and little squiggly bits like : and ; and ! so that it looks like a real book.

I am going to do the drawings! Lots of them. I like books with drawings. Sometimes I think it would be better if books didn't have anything *but* drawings. No words. Cat doesn't agree; she says you need both. I don't see why but, anyway I am going to do drawings instead of draggy descriptions that go on for ever and make you lose interest.

Like, for instance, I *could* say that Cat is...

Very tall and thin with lots of bony bits
and that she has:

a round jolly face

a wide mouth

sticky-out teeth

a blobby nose –
and that she wears:

eee-normous glasses

tight sweaters

short skirts

black tights

and long boots.

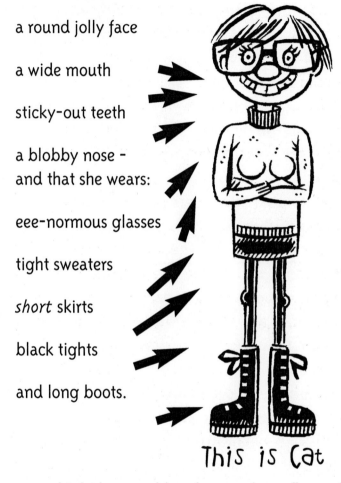

This is Cat

But I think that would make people go "Yawn!"
and not read any more. It's ever so much more fun
to draw!

I hope she doesn't mind me drawing her! I

can only do funny drawings. Even when I draw me I make me look funny. This is me:

All the drawings that I do, I'm putting with the tape so that Cat's mum knows where to leave a space when she does the typing. Then I will stick them on!

I still can't really understand why Cat wants me to record all this stuff. All about me and my boring life. When I asked her she said, "Well, look at it this way. It's not everyone can say they've written a book. Think what an achievement it would be!"

I said, "But nothing's ever happened to me." Meaning, I've never been kidnapped,

or lost at sea

or rescued anyone from drowning

or been in a plane that's been hijacked.

I have never been on a plane full stop. A BIG full stop.

I've never been abroad, I've never been on a boat, I've only been to the seaside once and that was two years ago when Nan gave us the money to go to Clacton and stay in a bed-and-breakfast. Even then it rained all the time. And Mum put some clothes to dry on the heater and the clothes caught fire while we were out and set light to the curtains and Dad got in a hump and spent all our money playing the fruit machines down the pub which meant we had to come home three days early and the bed-and-breakfast lady kept sending threatening letters about her curtains!

Nan and Grandy had to pay her in the end, to buy some new ones. Nan was ever so horrid about it. She said that Mum was like a child and that Dad was irresponsible and we didn't deserve to have holidays. So we've never had one since and now I don't suppose we'll ever have one again. See if I care!

That Tracey Bigg, she goes off all over the place. Places like Florida and Gran Canaria (wherever that is). She's always boasting about it. I haven't got anything to boast about. I just don't see what Cat wants me to say into this tape machine she's given me.

I said this to Cat and she chirruped, "Oh, Mandy, you've got all sorts of things!" Cat's always chirruping and chirping. She's ever such a cheerful person. So am I, I suppose, really. On the whole. Maybe that's why we're friends. She told me that things didn't have to be big and dramatic to be put into books.

"Just ordinary everyday happenings. That's what interests people."

Does she mean that other people are going to read about me???

I could be famous! I could be rich! They could make a film about me!

Yes, and if they do I know one person that's not going to be in it, and that's Tracey Bigg. If anyone gets to play her it'll be some ugly, cross-eyed, po-faced *tub*.

Serve her right! I can't stand that girl.

Chapter Two

This is her.

Tracey Bigg. She's always picking on me, just because she's Bigg and I'm Small. Which we really are. *Unfortunately.*

She's horrible! I hate her. She says these really mean and spiteful things just to try and hurt people. Like at the beginning of term when Miss Foster said we'd all got to read as many books as we could and get people to sponsor us, and the money we raised was going to go to charity, and Tracey Bigg sniggered and said, "What happens if we can't read, Miss?" and everyone knew she was talking about me.

Me and Oliver Pratt. Not that I cared, I don't care what anyone says, but Oliver went red as radishes and I felt really sorry for him. I mean, for all Tracey Bigg knows we've got that thing where you muddle your letters,* which is a sort of illness and nothing to do with being lazy or stupid. It's like being handicapped and people mocking at you.

Tracey Bigg is the sort of person that would mock at anyone that was handicapped. She'd kick a blind man's stick away from him just for fun, she would.

Tracey Bigg is garbage.

Miss Foster said that anyone that found reading difficult could choose books with pictures, but it didn't make any difference, I couldn't have found anyone to sponsor me anyway. I knew I couldn't ask Mum and Dad 'cos they were already worried about money, where is the next penny going to come from? and how are we going to pay all the bills? And I couldn't ask the neighbours 'cos Mum doesn't like me to do that. She says if I ask them, their kids will ask her, and then she'll feel embarrassed when she has to say no. And I could just imagine what would happen if I tried asking old Misery Guts!

*Note from Cat's mum: I think you mean "dyslexic" *Yes I do*

31

When it was time to give the forms back I had to pretend I'd lost mine. Miss Foster got really ratty with me. She said, "Mandy Small, what is the matter with you? You are the most careless, thoughtless child I have ever met!" And Tracey Bigg was there and she didn't half sneer. 'Cos she'd read more books than anyone, hadn't she? *And* made a load more money.

When we went into the playground at break she kept going on with this rhyme she'd made up.

> *"Mirror, mirror on the wall,*
> *who's the dumbest girl of all?*
> *Mandee! Mandy Small!"*

She taught it to Aimee Wilcox and Leanne Trimble that are her best friends and they went round chanting it all through break and doing this stupid dance that made everyone laugh.

I just took no notice. I mean, my
skin is really tough. It's like
I'm wearing body armour.
You could shoot arrows at it
and they'd just bounce off.
You could shoot bullets. You
could hurl dead elephants.

Tracey Bigg can't hurt *me*. But all the same, it does get on my nerves. You get to feeling like you're on the point of exploding. Like a bottle of fizzy pop that's been all shaken up and the cork is just about to b…*low*!

That's what happened back at half term. My cork just blew,

and I bopped her one. Actually, I bashed her. Right on the conk.

She bled gallons! She bled everywhere. All down her chin, drip-drip-drip. All down the front of her dress, drip-drop, drip-drop, *splodge*. What a mess! But it was her own fault. She asked for it. See, what happened, Miss Foster gave us these forms to take home. *More* forms. She's always giving us forms. Usually I just chuck mine away. I mean, I can't keep bothering Mum all the time. She'd only get fussed.

This lot was forms for going to summer camp. Down in Devon, on a farm.

"I don't expect most of you have ever been on a farm, have you?"

Tracey Bigg had. *Of course*. She's been everywhere. She's been to America. She's been to Australia. She's been to Switzerland and gone skiing in the mountains. She would!

I haven't ever been anywhere except to Clacton where it rained and Dad spent all our money. Oh, and to my nan's, but that's only a tube ride away. I would quite like to have seen a farm but I didn't think I could leave Mum and Dad for a whole fortnight even if Nan and Grandy offered to pay, which they might have done as on the whole they are quite generous. But I am always frightened that if I'm not there something disastrous will happen. Like I'll get back and find that Mum has burnt the house down or Dad's gone through the roof. Or even worse, that one of them has run away.

So I told Miss Foster I couldn't go and she seemed disappointed and said, "Oh, Mandy, that's a pity! I feel a change of scene would do you good."

I don't know what she meant by that. I don't need any change of scene! I'm quite happy where I am.

Anyway, out in the playground afterwards Tracey Bigg made up another of her stupid rhymes.

That was when I bashed her. And she yelled, and grabbed my hair, and tried to scratch my eyes out so I kicked her, really hard, on the ankle and she tore at my sleeve and that was when Miss Foster and another teacher came running across and separated us.

'Course, I got into dead trouble for that.

Dead trouble. Tracey said it was all my fault, and so did Aimee and Leanne. They said, "She attacked her, Miss."

Nobody ever asked me *why* I'd attacked her, and I wouldn't have told them even if they had. Not any of their business. But they didn't ever ask.

It's like I've got this reputation
        for being aggressive and
        Tracey's got this reputation
        for being *good* and that's
all anyone cares.
        But sometimes I
    think you have to
be a bit aggressive or people just
stamp all over you. Like with
Oliver, and Billy Murdo's gang.
They bully him something rotten and no one ever
does a thing about it. That's because they do it
where the teachers can't see. And Oliver, he's
such a sad, weedy little guy, he never sticks up
for himself.

I bet if he did, Miss Foster would say it was all
his fault, even though Billy Murdo's about ten
times bigger.

Sometimes you just can't win. But on the other
hand, you can't just sit back and do nothing. I
don't think you can.

Half-past three is when school ends. I can't
wait to get out! I never stay behind for anything;
not if I can help it. I run like a whirlwind to
Bunjy's to pick Mum up and go shopping
with her.

Bunjy's is the name of the baker's where Mum works. But the lady who owns it, the one who keeps threatening to give her the sack, isn't called Mrs Bunjy but Mrs Sowerbutts. Mum calls her old Sourpuss. She's not quite as bad as Misery Guts, but they both give Mum a lot of hassle.

Sometimes when I get there I'm a few minutes early. If old Sourpuss is around Mum pulls this face at me through the window and I know that I will have to wait.

Old Sourpuss wasn't there that day, the day I bashed Tracey Bigg and made her nose bleed. Mum came waltzing out looking all happy and giggly 'cos she'd left a few minutes before she ought!

I love it when Mum behaves like that. It means we're going to have *fun*!

Before we went home we called at the supermarket to buy some food for Dad's tea. Mum wanted to do him something different, something a bit posh. She started talking about making pastry and putting things inside it, but I managed to talk her out of *that* idea. Last time Mum tried making pastry it was an absolute disaster. It came out all hard, like a layer of cement. Dad said, "Blimey O'Reilly, you'd need a hammer and chisel to make any headway with this!"

I don't know why Dad says Blimey O'Reilly, but he only does it when he thinks something is funny. Sometimes he just doubles up laughing at Mum and her cooking. Once she put the sugar in the oven to dry and it melted all over the place, and Dad said she was daft as a brush. He said, "Oh, what a yum yum!" And we all fell about, including Mum.

But other times, like if he's had a bad day or old Misery's had a go at him, he doesn't say Blimey O'Reilly he says things that are cross and unkind and Mum gets all upset. So it seemed to me it was silly to take chances. I reckoned Mum ought to get him something he liked. Food is terribly important to men. They get really upset if they come home and their dinner isn't ready or it's not what they want. Women don't care quite so much. Well, that's how it seems to me.

So in the end we bought his favourite pie, which I reckoned even Mum couldn't ruin as all you have to do is just put it in the oven. Mum said, "We'll have toast fingers and a bit of paté to start with," 'cos she still wanted to be posh.

Well, we got in and first thing we know is old Misery Guts is there waiting for us, hiding behind the door. All in one breath she says, "Mrs-Small-I-really-must-complain-about-the-state-of-the-bathroom-it-looks-as-if-a-bomb-has-hit-it." To which Mum chirps, "We should be so lucky!" and goes racing up the stairs two at a time with me giggling behind her.

The reason the bathroom looked as if a bomb had hit it was that the hot water thingie had blown up when Dad was running his bath. The hot water thingie looks like an ancient monument.

Before you can get any hot water out of it you have to move lots of little levers and turn on lots of taps and then light a match. I'm not allowed to touch it in case I blow myself up. Half the wall is down, now.

"That Misery Guts," panted Mum, as we pounded up the stairs to our own floor. "A pity it couldn't have blown up when she was in there!"

"In the bath," I said.
"All naked."

Sometimes old Misery Guts makes Mum's life a real pain, but we just laughed about her that day. Mum was in a really giggly sort of mood. She turned the oven on, to heat it up for Dad's pie, and we had a cup of tea and watched a bit of telly, and then Mum put the pie in and I laid the table and we got the bread out for toasting.

"Let's do some thing special," said Mum. "Let's cut the toast into funny shapes. We'll cut one into a Misery Guts shape and see if your dad can guess who it is!"

So that was what we did. We made a Misery Guts shape and an old Sourpuss shape, and Mum made Nan and Grandy shapes, and I made Tracey Bigg and Miss Foster shapes, and then we just went mad and made any old shapes that took our fancy. Shapes with big heads, and shapes with big feet, and shapes with big bums. Fat shapes, skinny shapes. Tall shapes, short shapes. Shapes of all kinds!

old Sourpuss

misery guts

tracey bigg

We ended up with way too much toast!

"We've used up the whole loaf!" said Mum.

But we just giggled about it, 'cos that was the sort of mood we were in.

Dad got in at five o'clock. He swung me up in his arms and said, "And how's our Mand?"

"We've been making toasted teachers," I said.

"That sounds a bit dodgy," said Dad. "I hope they're not for my tea?"

"Only for starters," said Mum, proudly. She

was really chuffed with her posh starters. Paté and toast! That's what the nobs have.

"So what's for enders?" said Dad.

"Enders is trifle," I said. We'd bought some little pots of it at the supermarket.

"And middles?"

"Middles—"

"*Oh*!" Mum clapped her hand to her mouth. I ran for the oven. Too late! Dad's beautiful pie was ruined. We'd been so busy making toast shapes that Mum had forgotten to turn the oven down. The pie had burnt to a cinder!

I looked anxiously at Dad.

Dad said,
"What's this
supposed to be,
then? My tea?"

Mum, all tearful,
said, "There's
always baked beans."

"*Baked beans*?"
roared Dad. "I don't
want baked beans!' He banged with his fist on the table. "I want a man's meal, darling!"

I could see that any minute Mum was going to burst into tears, and I knew if she did that it would only get Dad even madder. So I rushed to put all the toast shapes on the table and said, "We could have baked beans on toasted teacher! Look, this one's Mr Phillpots, with his big bum! And this fat one is Mrs Duckworth. Or you could have beans on Misery Guts. This one's Misery Guts. See? Mum made her. 'Cos she moaned about the bathroom, so I reckon she deserves to get eaten. I think you should eat her and Mum should eat old Sourpuss. You could start with the head and work down. Or start at the feet and work up. Yum yum! Lovely bum!"

I'd picked out old Misery Guts and was pushing her at Dad and by this time he was laughing, and Mum was smiling a little tearful smile, so I knew that I could relax. Everything was going to be all right.

"Honest to God," said Dad, wiping his eyes, "I don't know where we'd be without you, Mand!"

My mum and dad really do *need* me.

I'm really enjoying telling my life story! I didn't think I would, I thought it would be a real drag. The only bit I was looking forward to was the drawings. But now I have discovered that I can put on different voices. Like for instance when I'm being Dad I put on this voice that is very grrrrrruff and

And when I'm being Mum I speak very high and light like soap bubbles.

Old Misery Guts, she's got a voice like a rusty tin full of nails. And when she speaks, her mouth goes like a prune.

So that's what I make my mouth go like when I'm being her.

Cat has a really **nice** voice. All warm and round and bubbly, like honey glugging out of a jar.

And she has this north country accent, which is fun.

If I'd have known I could do all these voices and act out being different people I could have been in our Christmas play. I could have played the lead instead of — guess who?

You've got it! Tracey Bigg. Aimee Wilcox said she was picked because she speaks nice. But I can speak nice! If I want to. I don't always want to. Anyway, I bet it wasn't 'cos she speaks nice, I bet it was 'cos she speaks
LOUD.
I can speak
loud.

Not that Miss Foster would pick me. She wouldn't ever. She reckons I'm useless and that my mum and dad are useless and that we're all a bunch of no-hopers. She won't half be surprised when my book's published!

Dad said the other day, "So! We're going to have a famous writer in the family, are we?"

I have thought about this, but while I would quite like to become famous (just to show Tracey Bigg and Miss Foster, and also, of course, to earn a lot of money) I don't think that I shall become famous by writing books. For one thing, I don't expect that Cat's mum would want to keep on typing them out for me. And for another, what would I write about??? Once I have told my life story, what is there left?

Maybe I will become a famous actress! Or a funny person on the telly, pretending to be well-known people. Taking them off. I bet I could do that! It would be a bit like Dad being Elvis.

I could be... Madonna!

I could be a Spice girl!

I could be the Queen!

I could be anyone!

Dad has heard me doing my voices. He'd really love to know what I'm talking about! He said, "You're not talking about us, are you, Mandy? Me and your mum? You're not giving our secrets away?"

Mum told him to let me alone. She said that I was doing it for Cat (only she calls her Miss Daley) and if Cat thought it was a good thing, "We oughtn't to interfere."

Dad said, "I'm not interfering, I just want to know what she's telling her."

He's tried wheedling and coaxing me, he's even tried bribing. He said, "Give you half a dollar if you'll let me have a listen!"

But I don't know what half a dollar is, and in any case what I'm talking about is strictly private.

strictly private

Well, almost strictly private. Just between me and Cat. And Cat's mum, of course, but I don't count her. She's only typing it out. It's not as if she knows us. She doesn't even live near us. She lives in Northwood, which is a dead posh area. We're nowhere near her. So I don't mind if she gets to hear what I'm saying, but no way do I want Dad to!

I was hoping, when I'd filled one tape, that Cat would say I could stop now, but she said, "Oh, no! You don't get let off that easily. I want a whole book out of you, young woman."

I said, "A whole *book*?" thinking that I would still be filling up tapes when I am old and ancient.

Cat said, "Well, several chapters at any rate."

I said, "How many is several?" and she said, "Mm… seven or eight?"

Seven or eight! I said, "I haven't lived long

enough to do seven or eight!" But Cat only laughed and said, "Get on with it, you're doing fine," and handed me another tape.

I suppose I don't mind, really.

Just so long as Dad doesn't get to eavesdrop!!!!

But I don't think he would.

Chapter Three

Here I am, starting over again. Testing, testing. One, two, three. This is Mandy Small telling her life story.

Now I'm going to play it back and see if it's come out OK.

Hearing your own voice is really strange! I don't sound a bit like what I thought I did. I thought I'd sound like someone on the television, maybe.

Talking posh.

Like Tracey Bigg.

Cat asked me once how I felt about Tracey Bigg. She said, "I get the feeling she upsets you."

She doesn't upset me! I'd just like to jump up and down on her a few times and squash her *flat*.

hi! this is mendy Small, tellin her laif story.

Then when I'd done it, I'd roll her up like an old carpet and stuff her in the bin.

I'm not supposed to be talking about Tracey Bigg. This book isn't about Tracey Bigg, it's about me! I don't know how she got into it again. She keeps getting into things. From now on I am going to *keep her out*.

That'll settle her.

Now I'm back to telling my life story, only I don't quite know what to tell. When I asked Cat, she said, "Just tell it like it is! Why not pick up where you left off?"

Where I left off was the night Mum burnt Dad's tea and we all ate toasted teacher and baked beans.

The next day was Saturday. I like Saturdays! They're one of my favourite days. *No school*, for one thing. For another, Mum doesn't have to work and neither does Dad.

Dad and I always go down the shops of a Saturday morning. Mum stops behind to catch up on stuff like the washing and the ironing. She has her treat on Sunday when she stays in bed. Sometimes she stays there until twelve o'clock! Sunday is Mum's day. But Saturday is mine and Dad's.

Dad was in a really good mood that particular Saturday. He fooled around doing his Elvis act as we walked down the road and Mrs Stern that lives at No. 4 called out to him.

"Hi, Barry! When we gonna see you down the *Hand & Flower* again?"

Mrs Stern is a huge fan of Dad's. She also does *a lot of drinking* in the *Hand & Flower*.

The *Hand & Flower* is where Dad fell off the stage in the middle of his Elvis gig. But Dad had not been drinking. He is just accident prone.

When we got to the shops Dad said, "Let's give your mum a surprise... let's go and buy some stuff to fix that kitchen cabinet she's always on about."

Mum had been on about the kitchen cabinet for weeks. *Months.* It's this little cupboardy thing that's supposed to be fixed to the wall only one day it went and fell down right on top of me and almost knocked me out.

I didn't half see stars!

I had to go to the hospital and have a chunk of hair cut off and six stitches, and I had this enormous great lump like a football stuck out the side of my head.

I told Miss Foster I'd slipped on the ice (it was way back last winter and it was really cold). I thought it sounded silly to say a kitchen cabinet had fallen on me.

Like one time when the banister rail broke and I fell down the stairs and twisted my ankle, Miss Foster looked at me like she just couldn't believe people lived in houses where that sort of thing happened. But our house is really old and it crumbles all the time. Just at the moment there was this rotten floor board on the landing. It had got rotted 'cos of rain coming through the roof. Old houses always have leaky roofs; even ones that belong to dukes and duchesses.

I don't know if they have cupboards that come off the walls.

Mum and Dad had a right old row about that cupboard 'cos Mum had been telling Dad for ages it was going to come down.

"We'll fix it for her," said Dad. "Be like a sort of birthday treat."

"But Mum's already had her birthday," I said.

Dad said OK, it would be an *in-between* birthday treat.

"And while I'm about it, I'll knock down that wardrobe and make a shelf for you."

Well, at least we bought the stuff for doing it with. Some things to hold it up and things for fixing it to the wall. I mean, it was a start. It was closer than he'd ever come before.

"I'll do it," said Dad. "You'll see."

I really thought that this time he might, but I wasn't surprised when he didn't. I know my dad! He means well, but he gets very easily sidetracked.

Like on the way back from the D.I.Y. store he wanted to get side-tracked into the betting shop, only I wouldn't let him.

Last time he got sidetracked in the betting shop he put all the housekeeping money on a horse called *Sweet Sandy Star*, on account of Star being my mum's name before she got married. Dad said it was such a terrific coincidence that the horse simply couldn't lose. Only it did. It came in last. Dad's horses always do. So after that he gave me strict instructions: "You're not to let me go into that betting shop ever again. Understand? I'm relying on you, girl!"

It is rather a responsibility, but it made Mum really upset when he lost all the housekeeping money. We had to beg from Nan, and Mum hates doing that.

When he's in a good mood Dad actually thanks me for stopping him. That's what he did that Saturday. He ruffled my hair and said, "Good old Mand! Keeping her dad on the straight and narrow." And then he said was he allowed to just buy a couple of lottery tickets, and I said yes, because you never know, you *could* win a million pounds, it's just that I have to be there with him or he'll start buying scratch cards like there's no tomorrow and that's almost as bad as the horses. The thing is with Dad, he can't help himself. Like Mum can't help doing some of the daffy things she does.

They need me to look after them.

Mum was so pleased when Dad and I got home without spending the housekeeping money! Dad said, "You've got Mand to thank for that. She's my guardian angel, aren't you, poppet?" And then he showed Mum all the stuff that we'd got at the D.I.Y. All the screws and the hinges and things to make holes with and the things to put into the holes once they'd been made, and Mum said, "Oh! You're never going to fix that kitchen cabinet at last?" Dad just grinned and said, "Only if you behave yourself."

He didn't do the cabinet that afternoon because of sport on the telly. Dad's a huge sports fan! He'll watch anything, even snooker. Mum and I don't care for it, so I went into my room to do some more tape for Cat, and Mum went over the road to her friend Deirdre that's just had a new baby.

Sometimes I think that Mum would quite like a new baby herself, but I expect Nan's right and it wouldn't be sensible. I bet I know who'd end up looking after it if she did have one! Not that I'd mind; I think babies are cute. When I grow up I'm going to have at least six. Both sexes. Maybe triplets, then I could get it over with in just two goes.

Of course I would have to find a husband first, and that might not be so easy as at the moment I happen to think that boys are the pits. We have a *lot* at our school.

They are all disgusting. Maybe they get better as they grow older. I can only hope!

When Mum came back from seeing the new baby she said to Dad, "What do you want for your tea?" and Dad said, "Something special," and I saw Mum start to look worried 'cos I knew that all she'd got was fish fingers or egg and chips (which as a matter of fact are two of my all-time favourite meals). Then Dad jumped up and switched off the telly and said, "Let's go out! It's time we treated ourselves."

Mum got as far as saying, "But what about the—"

Gas bill, probably. Or the electricity. A bill of some kind. But when Dad gets an idea in his head there's no stopping him. He simply pulled Mum towards him and planted this huge smacker of a kiss on her lips and roared, "Forget it! Whatever it is. Forget it! I'm tired of counting every penny! I want a good time!"

So Mum went and got dressed up in her best pink skirt and this lovely slinky blouse that has pictures of pop stars all over it, and Dad put on his best denims and his Levi jacket, and slicked his hair back like Elvis, and we went trolling up the road to the Indian restaurant.

I feel really proud of my mum and dad when they get all their gear on! If you didn't know, you'd think probably they were on the telly, or celebrities of some kind. Mum was still going on a bit about the bills (I think Nan scared her when they had to ask for help with the electric) but Dad said —

I can't say what he really said as Cat's mum might not like it! I expect where she lives in Northwood they don't say things like ••••.*

And it was fun, to begin with. It always is, to begin with. I always hope that it will go on being, and sometimes it does and that is wonderful. I mean, that is just absolutely THE BEST.

I kept my fingers crossed that that was how it would be that night.

Just at first, I thought it might. Dad picked

* Note from Cat's mum: I'm afraid they do, but you're quite right, I don't like it.

up the menu and said, "Now, Mand, you can have just whatever you like." So I started off with poppadoms and chutney, and then I had samosas, with mint sauce, and then I had a biryani, and then I had an ice cream, bright green with little coloured bits all over it: only by the time I got to the ice cream, things weren't being such fun any more as Mum and Dad were having one of their rows.

Dad accused Mum of being a misery and a killjoy, and Mum accused Dad of being irresponsible. She said that it was Nan's fault, she said she'd spoilt him, and Dad said, "You leave my mum out of this!" and before I knew it they were at it hammer and tongs.

They say such terrible things when they get angry. Like, "I don't know why I ever married you" and "You're nothing but a millstone round my neck." The sort of things that make me terrified they won't want to go on living together. I couldn't bear it if my mum and dad split up! I know Nan says they're useless, the pair of them, but they're my mum and dad and I love them!

What made things worse was that Mum was drinking too much wine. She's all right if she just has one glass, but if she has more than one it makes her tearful. And if she has more than *two* it makes her tipsy. She doesn't get drunk or throw up or anything horrid like that. She just gets a bit wobbly and out of control and then the wine gets spilt and the glasses get smashed and Dad says she's a liability and that he can't take her anywhere.

I tried to stop her. I said, "Mum, if you have any more you'll only get tipsy," but she wouldn't listen to me. She was going on about the telephone bill and how the telephone people had sent a nasty letter saying they were going to cut us off and how she wasn't going to go to Nan for help, not this time, not ever again, "Because she's so hateful to me, she always seems to think it's my fault!"

Dad said well, it was. He said Mum was the one who was supposed to buy the stamps for the telephone bill; why hadn't she bought them? And Mum poured another glass of wine and started crying and saying how could she buy them when Dad insisted on throwing money away on Indian meals when he could have stayed at home and had fish fingers?

To which Dad snarled that he couldn't stand

another day of Mum's cooking, she couldn't even cook a fish finger without ruining it.

And I knew what was going to happen, so I just took out my pen and some paper, which I always carry with me, and started doing some drawings and tried not to listen.

But you can't not listen as they always drag you into it.

It's always like this. It's very embarrassing, in the middle of a restaurant. Both of them wanting to know that I love them best. I love them equally! I love them both *so much*. I wish they wouldn't fight! I really really do!

It is a good thing that Balji, who owns the restaurant, is used to my mum and dad. When Dad went storming off to the loo and Mum reached out a hand and sent her wine spilling all over the table and just sat there weeping, he came over immediately with a cloth and very calmly began to mop it all up.

I said, "I think we'd better have the bill, now, Balji," and Balji nodded and said, "And a cab?" I said, "Yes, please. And a cab."

He always gets us a cab. Well, I mean, not *always*. Mum and Dad don't *always* have rows in his restaurant. Mum doesn't *always* start weeping. But it has happened quite often. I always pray that it won't, but Mum does worry so about how the bills are going to be paid and Dad does so hate to be nagged. If we just had a bit more money, things would be all right.

By the time we got home Mum had stopped crying and Dad had stopped threatening to walk out and they were both sitting there in front of the telly so I thought it would be safe to leave them. So I went to bed and said my special prayer and I had just about fallen to sleep when I was woken by the horrible voice of old Misery Guts shrieking up the stairs.

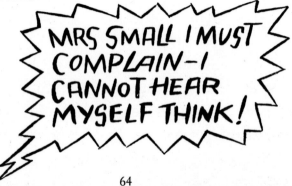

MRS SMALL I MUST COMPLAIN – I CANNOT HEAR MYSELF THINK!

Mum and Dad were at it again. Bickering and bawling at each other in the sitting-room.

I threw back the duvet and went tearing into the sitting-room. I was in such a rush I forgot all about the broken floorboard on the landing. My foot went right through it.

At least it stopped them fighting. So I guess it was worth it.

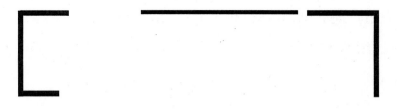

Cat's mum has typed out the whole of my first tape! She must type incredibly fast. About 100mph, I should think.

Phew! I can't imagine how anyone could move their fingers that quick. And no crossings-out, or anything. It's as neat as neat, just like a real book.

I wonder who will publish it? If anyone! I can't think who would be interested in the life story of someone like me. Cat says, "People who have the same sort of problems, that's who."

What does she mean, problems? I don't have problems! Cat seems to think that Mum and Dad are a problem, but they are not. Only when they quarrel, because that is upsetting, but they have promised they will not do it any more.

They *say* they have turned over a new leaf.

It would be nice if they didn't — quarrel, I mean — but I expect they will. It's when things get on top of them and Dad spends all the money and Mum does something daft. But so long as I am there to keep an eye on them they will always, hopefully, kiss and make up.

Oh ho ho!

Cat says it must be a great responsibility for me. She says, "It's a very grown up sort of thing to do, Mandy." Well, so maybe I'm a very grown up sort of person! I don't see what's wrong with that. Cat says what's wrong is that I should be enjoying myself and doing all the things that other kids do. *I* say, suppose I don't want to do the things that other kids do? I can still enjoy myself! It's not a problem for me to keep an eye on my mum and dad. It would only be a problem if we stopped being together as a family. But that is why I say my special prayer every night.

When I tell this to Cat she says, "That's what I mean about people who would be interested in reading about you. You're not the only one who worries about their mum and dad getting divorced. I'm afraid it happens all the time."

I said, "I'm not really worried." Not if I go on saying my prayer. My mum and dad couldn't get divorced! How would one of them manage without me?

All the same, it did make me stop and think. Imagine if there are thousands of other people just like me, all worrying — *really* worrying — and saying their prayers. Perhaps they would read my book and think, "Oh, that girl is just like me. I know just how she feels." And it would be a comfort to them to know that they are not the only ones. That is what Cat says.

So maybe somebody *will* publish it, after all! And then I will be famous and make lots of money, which I will give to Mum and Dad so that we can move to a proper house where the floorboards don't collapse and there is a bathroom all of our own and they will not quarrel any more. That, at least, is my dream. Tracey Bigg will be just so-o-o-o jealous!

Oh! I have just had a thought. Suppose she tries to sue me for that thing that people are always suing the newspapers for? When they say things that aren't true?*

But I am only saying things that *are* true. So sucks to Tracey Bigg!

*Note from Cat's mum: Libel? **Yes!**

I'm really glad I didn't go on that summer camp. Two weeks with Tracey Bigg! Yeeeeeurgh!!!

Cat asked me the other day if I had any friends at school. I haven't, but who needs them? I've got my mum and dad!

Cat said, "You ought to have friends of your own age, Mandy." I don't see why. I did have a friend, once. She was called Janis and she was really nice. She lived next door and we used to play together. She had to be in a wheelchair 'cos there was something wrong with her legs, and I used to gallop her up and down the street.

One time she fell out, but she didn't mind. She just laughed!

She was ever so sparky, Janis was. Even though she couldn't walk, we still had fun.

Then the Social came and moved her, her and her mum, 'cos they said their accommodation was *sub-standard*, meaning it was like ours, all damp and fungussy and falling to pieces, so now they're on an estate and it's miles away, miles and miles, and I never see her. But she was my friend.

There isn't anyone at school I would want to be friends with. They all think I'm a retard. Tracey Bigg said once that I ought to be in a special unit.

Wait until I've had my book published! Then she'll change her tune.

That'll show her!

Chapter Four

Sunday was one of the best days. We had a really good time on Sunday! A *really* good time. Mum and Dad didn't quarrel once. It was one of those extra special days when just everything goes right.

It started with me and Dad making Mum's breakfast and Dad taking it in to her, all on a tray, all proper, with a tea towel and all.

We did:

Dad said, "Here you are, Moddom! Room service!" Mum sat up in bed in her nightie and went, "Ooh! A Sunday treat!"

Dad said, "We're spoiling you, 'cos we love you. Don't we, Mandy?"

And then, guess what? He went out to the

kitchen and came back with the frying pan, pretending to be Elvis!

He sang Mum's favourite, *Love me Tender*. It made them go all spoony, so I finished off the toast.

After breakfast, we did the washing-up. Together! Me and Dad! Usually Dad won't do the washing-up, he says it's a woman's job. This is because he never had to do it when he was a boy, and why Mum says he's been spoilt. Nan is incredibly old-fashioned. It's weird because she was around in the Swinging Sixties and so you would think she would be rather swinging herself, but she isn't at all. It would be hard to imagine anyone less swinging than my nan!

I think Grandy might have been a bit of a swinger, if Nan would have let him.

But Nan keeps a tight rein. That is what Mum says.

Mum says that if she didn't, Grandy would most likely "break out".

But I don't think he could run very far, at his age!

After Dad and I had washed up, I came into my bedroom to do some more tape, leaving Dad in the kitchen surrounded by all his bits and pieces from the D.I.Y. He was going to fix the cabinet at last!

I'd been in here for about ten minutes when there was a knock at the door and Dad peered round. He said, "How much?" I said, "How much for what?" Dad said, "For letting me have a listen! How much'll it take?" I said, "*Da-a-ad,*" and threw one of my pillows at him.

Dad said, "Oh, come on, Mand! None of that prissy missy stuff with me!"

I told him it wasn't prissy, it was PRIVATE. "Like a diary."

"You mean, you can't be bought?" said Dad.

I said, "No, I can't!" and hurled my other pillow at him.

"Spoilsport!" said Dad, as he chucked it back at me.

The next minute I crept over to the door and heard the sound of a drill whizzing in the kitchen, so I knew he'd just been trying it on. All the same, I have found a safe place to keep this tape! This is where I'm keeping it.

I don't think Dad would ever do anything behind my back, but he is *dead* curious to know what I'm saying!

By the time Mum got up to do the dinner, the kitchen cabinet was back on the wall. Mum was ever so pleased! She threw her arms round Dad's neck and gave him the hugest kiss ever.

Dad grinned and said, "Will I get one like that from you, Mandy, when I do your bedroom shelf? Or maybe you'll let me have a listen to that tape, instead…"

Dead curious!

He didn't get around to doing my shelf that afternoon as Mum's friend Deirdre came over with her husband and her baby. The baby's name is Felix. He is really sweet! He has the darlingest smile and these tiny little hands with an amazingly strong grip.

Deirdre said I could hold him if I wanted, so I took him on a guided tour of the room, showing him things and giving them to him to hold, only most of the time he wanted to put them in his mouth!

After we'd been all round the room, I sat with him on my lap, and then I said to Deirdre that I thought maybe his nappy needed changing – it was just this strange feeling that I had! – and so we went into the kitchen and I was right, he'd gone and pooped himself with all the excitement. I suppose to some people it might have seemed a bit yucky and pongy, but he's only a teeny baby, after all, and it is quite natural, so that it didn't bother me one little bit. I even helped Deirdre to change him! When we got back to the sitting-room she said to Mum, "Your Mandy is quite a little mother already."

Mum said, "Yes, I expect she'd like a brother or sister of her own, wouldn't you, Mand?"

Quickly, because *someone* has to be responsible in this family, I said, "Yes, but only when my book is published and I have made a lot of money and we can move into a proper house. I think we ought to wait until then, otherwise where would it sleep?"

Everyone seemed to find this rather amusing, I can't think why, but grown-ups do tend to laugh at the strangest things. Dad said, "Wait until you have a book published? Stone me! We'll be waiting for ever! How do you expect to write a book when you don't ever read any?"

"My tapes," I said. "They're going to be one."

Dad said, "Oh! Your tapes." And then to Deirdre and her husband, whose name is Garry, he said, "She's making these top-secret tapes that I'm not allowed to listen to."

Garry said, "Quite right! How can she slag you off if she knows you're going to be breathing down her neck?"

I said, "I'm not slagging him off! I wouldn't ever slag my dad off." And then I looked at Felix, back in his mum's arms, and I said, "I'm going to have six babies when I grow up."

Everybody laughed – *again* – except Dad, who said, "You're a bit young to be thinking of that sort of thing."

"She can dream," said Garry.

"The only problem is," I said, "finding the right man."

"That's all our problems," said Deirdre.

"Boys are just so *grungy*," I said.

Later in the afternoon we all went down the road to the park, where there was a fair going on. Oliver and his mum were there. Oliver and me waved at each other as we passed. Oliver called out, "Hi, Mandy! I'm having fun!" When we'd gone on a bit Deirdre said, "Who was that strange little chap? He looked like a turnip!"

I said, "That's very unfair to turnips," and everyone laughed, but afterwards I felt mean and wished I hadn't said it. Everyone laughs at Oliver.

Dad had seen a coconut shy. They had all these coconuts wearing politicians' masks and Dad couldn't wait to go and throw things at them!

We were just making our way over there when Garry caught my arm and said, "Hey, look at that, Mand!" and pointed to where there was this notice announcing:

Mum and Deirdre immediately wanted me to have a go, but I couldn't think what I could do. (I didn't know then that I could put on voices or maybe I'd have been the Queen or someone.)

It was Dad who told me to sing a song. He said, "Go on! What about that one Grandy taught you? One about the dustman?" Garry said, "Yeah! Brilliant!" and he and Dad marched me over to the person that was in charge and got him to write my name down on a list and I just didn't know how to get out of it. I thought perhaps Mum might tell Dad to stop being so daft – I mean *me*, singing! – but she seemed just as keen as he was. She kept saying, "Imagine if you won!"

I was quite nervous when my turn came 'cos lots of the other kids had been really good and nobody had sung a song like Grandy's dustman song. But Deirdre said, "Sock it to 'em, baby!"

and Dad gave me a little push, and before I knew it I was out there, in front of everyone, and this man was introducing me as "Miss Mandy Small, who is going to sing for us."

This is the song that I sang:

"My old man's a dustman
He wears a dustman's hat
He wears cor blimey trousers
And he lives in a council flat.

He looks a proper 'nana
In his great big hobnail boots
He's got such a job to pull them up
He calls them daisy roots."

CLUMP! CLUMP!

And I did this clumping dance to go with it, which made everyone laugh.

I'd never done the dance before. It just, like came to me all of a sudden, and so I did it.

I don't expect it's the sort of song that Cat's mum would approve of* but people clapped and clapped and guess what? I got third prize!!! It was a CD of Oasis, which was a pity in a way as we don't have a CD player but Deirdre does, so I gave it to her to keep for me and she said I could go over and play it whenever I liked. So far I've played it about fifty times!

After the talent competition Oliver came up to us with his mum and said he thought I should have won first prize, not third. He said he was going to tell everyone at school about it only of course he didn't, did he? He forgot. And I couldn't very well go round telling people myself, so Tracey Bigg never got to hear. I'd like to have seen the expression on *her* face if she'd seen me winning a prize!

Anyway, Mum then decided she had to have a go at something so she went to this stall where you had to throw hoops over pegs 'cos there was a teddy bear she was desperate for. She tried and tried, but she couldn't get the hoops anywhere near, so in the end Dad said, "Let me have a go," and he won it for her! A huge great big teddy bear! Mum wanted to give it to me, to make up for the CD that I'd had to give to Deirdre, but

*Note from Cat's mum: Nonsense! It's great fun.

Dad wouldn't let her. He said, "No way, Sand!" He sounded quite hurt about it. He said, "I got it for *you*." So Mum kept it and now it sits on her pillow and she calls it Dumpling. I don't mind about not having it. I'm too old for teddy bears!

We stayed in the park till nearly eight o'clock. We ate burgers and fries and iced donuts, and Garry bought me candy floss, and I saw a girl from school and wondered if she'd heard me singing in the talent competition (which she obviously hadn't or if she had she never mentioned it). Altogether it was a lovely, lovely day and one that I shall remember for ever. When I am old and grey like Nan I will still be telling my grandchildren about it, about me winning third prize and singing *My Old Man's a Dustman*. And maybe I will croak my way through it and do the little dance and they will look at me and think, "Poor old Nan! She's past it." But I won't care! 'Cos I will still have the memory.

When we got home, Deirdre and Garry came in for a cup of coffee and we all sat and watched the telly and I was allowed to stay up till almost midnight. This is something my nan thinks is terrible, a child being allowed to stay up. But Mum and Dad always let me, if anything exciting is going on. They don't really mind what time I go to bed. Dad says, "She's not stupid. She'll go when she's tired." And I do, as a rule, but that night I was having too good a time!

Deirdre wanted to see the floorboard before she left. She knew about it 'cos of my black eye. She said, "You'd better show me. I don't want to go falling through it." But Dad told her it was all right, it was further along the landing, and anyway he'd roped it off.

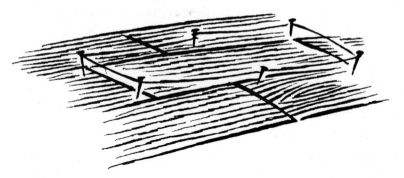

We all stood, gazing at the floorboard.
"Oh, that's really classy, that is," said Garry.
Poor Dad looked quite crestfallen!

Next day was Monday. Ugh! I hate Mondays. Mondays mean *school*.

It was the last week before the summer holidays and I begged and begged Mum to let me stay at home. I looked such a sight!

How could I tell Miss Foster I'd fallen through a floorboard? I'd just be  so embarrassed! She'd already heard about the kitchen cabinet falling on me and the banisters breaking. Miss Foster doesn't understand about old houses. She lives in a modern flat. She doesn't realise that old houses are always a bit crumbly.

But anyway I had to go 'cos Mum said it would be breaking the law if I didn't and Mum's dead scared of breaking the law. She said, "Nobody's going to laugh at you."

Huh! That's all she knew.

Tracey Bigg laughed like a *drain*.

Miss Foster said, "Dear me, Mandy! In the wars again? What happened this time?" I told her that I'd fallen down the stairs, and old Tracey, she pulls this face, as if to say, "She would!" and afterwards, when I go into the playground, she's waiting for me with her gang and she's made up another of her stupid rhymes.

She needn't think *I* care.

I've been thinking what sort of house we'll buy when my book is published and we have lots of money.

It's got to be a real house, not just rooms in someone else's. And it's got to have a garden, so that I can grow flowers.

This is the sort of house I think we'll have.

And it won't be in London! It will be somewhere nice, like Croydon. My Uncle Allan and Auntie Liz live in Croydon. They live in Linden Close, and it's really beautiful.

Uncle Allan is Dad's brother. He has done well

for himself, my nan says. He is a manager in Sainsbury's, and that, I think, pays more money than being a window cleaner. But I bet my dad could be a manager in Sainsbury's if he wanted! He just doesn't want, that's all.

When we have our house it will be like Uncle Allan's, in a nice road that is all quiet, with trees and grass. And it will have a name, such as Sky View or The Laurels or Mandalay. Mandalay, I think, is pretty. There is a house near us called Mandalay. When I was little I used to think it said Mandy!

We will definitely have a house; it is the first thing we will get.

Another thing we will have is a car. Everybody has a car. Even Deirdre and Garry have one, though it is what Dad calls a banger, meaning it is clapped out and you can hear it coming from streets away.

We will have a better car than that! A little one because they are sweet, and also they would not use so much petrol.

We are the only people I know who don't have a car (apart from Misery Guts, but she is too old). It is all right for Tracey Bigg going on about the ecology and how cars are poisoning the planet, but her mum has a *whacking* great huge one which she comes and picks her up in after school. It is a real gas guzzler.

Our little baby car will only need a tiny drop.

Anyway, I can't say I've ever noticed Tracey walking home to save the planet being poisoned. She jumps into the car quick enough. She's all mouth, that girl is.

I have made up a rhyme about *her*.

> *Tracey Bigg goes "Wah-wah-wah"*
> *When she talks it's all blah-blah*
> *She's a stupid steaming nit*
> *Posho loudmouth bighead twit.*

If I knew how to spell it I'd chalk it up on one of the lavatory walls.

I will know how to spell it when Cat's mum has typed it out. Ho ho! You just watch it, Tracey Bigg!

Chapter Five

Hi! It's me again. Back on line, doing my life story. I've been working on it for ages, now. Ever since Cat first suggested it, which was way back months ago.

I aim to finish it pretty soon. I asked Cat when she wanted it done by, and she said, "Well, just as soon as you can manage." What she means is, I should get it all down before I go completely fruit and nutty.

I *will* be fruit and nutty, before very long. Just as I think I've got my mum and dad sorted, they go and do something else totally mad and daft and irresponsible. It's like they are both completely *off the wall*.

I hoped after I fell through the floorboard we'd have a bit of peace and quiet in the Small household. I mean, the hot water heater had already blown up, so that couldn't happen again. The floorboard had been roped off, and so had the banisters; I just couldn't see what else there was that could go wrong. But trust my mum and dad! They'll always find something.

First thing that happens, Dad gets out of bed in the early hours of the morning and forgets about the floorboard and goes and treads on one of the nails he's knocked in to stop people falling through. He doesn't half yell!

He yells so loud that even Mum wakes up. Her and me come rushing out, and a door opens somewhere down below and old Misery Guts starts shrieking up the stairs.

Dad's got this big hole in his foot and he's in agony, dancing up and down. Mum bathes it for him but we haven't got any Dettol, only household cleaner, and he won't let her use that. I say what about if I go down to the garden and get some mud, 'cos I've heard that if you put mud on to wounds it helps them heal, but he won't let me do that, either.

He bawls, "What's your game? For crying out loud! I could lose my leg!"

Misery Guts then joins in with "Mr-Small-do-you-mind-I-am-trying-to-get-some-sleep!" to which Dad shouts

something a bit rude and goes limping back to bed, and I lie awake all the rest of the night wondering what we'd do if he really lost his leg and thinking that I've got to finish this book, quick, and get some money in case he can't clean windows any more.

So that's the first crazy thing that happens. The second thing is that I meet Mum at Bunjy's after school and she's dead set on going off to buy some paint that will glow in the dark so's we can paint the floorboard and Dad won't be able to tread on it by mistake any more. So we get this paint, it's bright yellow, and we go rushing home with it all happy, and we have a cup of tea and a bit of a watch of the telly, 'cos there's this programme Mum really likes called *Carrot Tops* (it's for kids, really. But it is quite funny). Then Mum sends me down the road for some fish and chips while she gets on and paints the floorboard.

When I come back Mum's yanked out all Dad's nails and the floorboard's gleaming bright yellow like a fried egg yolk. It hits you the minute you get to the top of the stairs. It kind of YELLS at you.

"Nobody could miss seeing *that*," says Mum, proudly.

But guess what?

You've got it! Dad misses it.

Actually, he goes and puts his foot right in it.

So now we have yellow blobs all along the landing.

My family!

Next thing I know it's morning and I have to go to school again, and I've still got my black eye and Tracey Bigg's still doing her stupid song and dance act, but I don't take any notice. Oliver's in the corner of the playground crying 'cos Billy

Murdo's gang's duffed him up, so I go over and talk to him and try to put a bit of stuffing into him.

I say, "What's the problem?" and he goes, "*Blub – hic – sniffle* – Billy – *blub – hic* – hurt – *sniffle* – me." I feel sorry for him 'cos he's ever so harmless and they just pick on him all the time. They *torment* him. They're real bullies. There just isn't any way poor old Oliver can get back at them. He's just not that sort of person. I mean, if Tracey Bigg and her mob tried to duff me up I'd give them what for, I can tell you. I'd knee them and crunch them and use Kung Fu like on the telly.

I certainly wouldn't go into a corner and blub. But Oliver is ever so pathetic and weedy. I guess he just can't help it.

People that beat up on weeds are despicable.

It's the last day of term and tomorrow everyone except me and Oliver and a couple of others are going off to summer camp so for a treat Cat takes me and Oliver on a special trip, just the two of us.

We get on the tube and go to Mile End, where there's this museum that's a real old Victorian school. Cat says, "It'll show you what it would have been like to be Victorian children."

Oliver and me look at each other and giggle. I don't quite know why we giggle. Maybe it's just the excitement of being out of school, on our own, with Cat. If it was an ordinary school trip I'd be expecting to be a bit bored. I mean, a *museum*. All full of dead stuff, and things from the past. I'm not interested in the past! But as we're with Cat I think maybe it might be fun, 'cos I can't imagine Cat ever doing anything that's boring.

Oliver says to me, "When's Victorian?" and I'm not sure. I say, "Oh! About... a hundred years ago." And I'm right! Cat says that Queen Victoria died in 1901. I know more history than I thought!

The museum isn't a bit like I think it's going to be. I think it's going to be very large and gloomy with glass cases full of dead stuff, but all it is, it's just this old grungy building with nothing in it, except when you go up the stairs you suddenly find yourself in a schoolroom, with all desks and benches, just like it would have been in Victorian times. There's even a teacher, wearing a white frilly blouse and a long black skirt with her hair pulled into a bun. She's standing at a blackboard with this long stick that Cat says is called a pointer.

There's other children there besides us. They're all sitting down, waiting for the class to begin, so me and Oliver sit at the back, next to each other, in this funny sort of desk that's like two desks joined together.

It's really ancient, you can tell. The wood's all worn and stained, and there's loads of names and initials carved into the top.

Cat whispers, "Imagine! Some of these were done by children over a hundred years ago."

It makes me feel a bit shivery when I think about a girl the same age as me sitting where I'm sitting, resting her elbows on the desk lid just like I am, *a hundred years ago*. She'd have sat there never guessing that one day I'd be in her seat, trying to picture what she was like. I look at the names and initials and think that she could have been Eliza, or Jane, or "SW" or Grace. She'd be dead by now, of course. She'd have had her life. I've still got all mine to come!

I think it's good, sometimes, to remember about people from the past and wonder what they would have been like. The answer is – just the same as us, only different!

Not different *inside* themselves; just outside. I expect Eliza or Jane or whatever she was called would have understood about Tracey Bigg and how she gets on my nerves. She might even have had her own Tracey Bigg. Except she probably wouldn't have been called Tracey, because I don't think people were. Not in those days. She'd have been called... Henrietta. Henrietta Bigg! And Eliza Small. And they'd have made up rude and revolting rhymes about each other just like me and Tracey.

Well, that's what I like to imagine.

When everyone's sitting at their desks, the teacher announces that the first lesson is going to begin. Oliver looks at me, and I can see that he's a bit apprehensive. Oliver's not very good at lessons. Nor am I, usually, but today, surprise surprise, I turn out to be THE STAR!

The first lesson's arithmetic. We all have to sit with straight backs and chant our tables, right through to twelve.

I know them all! And my voice is the
L.O.U.D.E.S.T!

The next lesson is writing, with pen and ink.
The old desks have inkwells with real ink in them,
and the teacher gives us all a wooden pen with a
funny scratchy nib and a sheet of something
called blotting paper. The blotting paper's thick
and white and it blots the ink so's it doesn't
smudge.

The teacher writes the letters of the alphabet
on the board in beautiful curly shapes and we all
have to copy them. Cat says the shapes are
"copperplate" and they're the way Victorian
children had to write.

The idea is to do them without any splotches or
mess. I do mine really well! Not a single splotch!
When we've copied all the letters off the board

we have to write our names in the same sort of writing. This is mine:

Mandy Small

The teacher says mine is the best! She even hands it round for people to look at. And then she gives me a gold star and writes 10/10 in red ink. So I feel really pleased and think that things are looking up, what with me winning a prize in the talent competition and now getting a gold star for writing my name in copperplate. It's a pity Oliver can't get one, too, but his copperplate is all blotched and drippy.

O.liver.

Cat says it doesn't matter. She says the idea was that we should enjoy ourselves, and in any case I don't think Oliver really minds all that much. When Cat asks him if he's had a good time he gives her this big goofy grin and says yes, he'd like to go to a Victorian school every day "and sit next to Mandy in a big desk".

He's so funny, Oliver is. I quite like him really, I suppose. He can't help being a weed.

When we get back to school Cat says she's got something for me, and it's all the pages of my life story that her mum has typed out! She gets me to read bits of it and I'm really surprised at some of the long words I'd used. Without even realising!

The only trouble is, some of them are so long I can't read them. Imagine! Not being able to read your own life story!

I'm really worried about this. I ask Cat if she thinks I'm that *word*. The one her mum said. *Dys-*something. The one that means you get your letters muddled up. But Cat says she doesn't think I am. She says, "Just a bit slow at getting the hang of it." Before I can stop myself I say, "Just a bit *slow*." Cat gets really cross. She does what my nan calls "bristling".

She says, "No, I do *not* mean 'just a bit slow'. You're a bright girl, Mandy. Why do you keep putting yourself down all the time?"

I tell her that I don't *all* of the time. Just some of the time. And I don't want to grow up with everyone still sneering and jeering at me 'cos I can't read!

Cat promises me that this won't happen. She tells me about her brother, who was just like me when he was my age, but one day, quite suddenly, bingo! He discovered he could do it.

"And now he's at college, training to be a teacher."

I don't mean to be rude but I can't help pulling a

face when she says this 'cos a teacher is just about the last thing I'd want to be. Imagine having to teach someone like Tracey Bigg! So Cat asks me what I'd like to be, and I say maybe an actress or someone that does funny voices and makes people laugh. And then I tell her that what I'd really like would be to go to an acting school, if only I had the money. I say, "Maybe after my book's published I will have. Maybe it will make my fortune."

Cat looks a bit anxious when I say this. She explains to me that it is not easy for anyone to get a book published. She says, "It will still be a wonderful achievement whether it's published or not. But I don't want to give you false hopes. I'd hate you to be disappointed."

I won't be disappointed! I can tell the difference between what's real and what's just pretend. It's a game I play. "When my book is published." I know it won't be *really*. Probably not. But I can dream, can't I?

After school's broken up and we've all been set free I go and meet Mum from Bunjy's and show her my copperplate. Mum says the copperplate is beautiful. And then she looks at the blotting paper, which the teacher said I could bring with me, and she takes out her mirror and shows me how you can read the writing that's on it.

Mandy Small

Like a secret code!

When we get home old Misery's on the prowl. She's found a dob of yellow paint on the hall floor and she wants to know how it got there. Mum says, "Oh, dear, it must have dropped off the brush when I leaned over the banisters," and old Misery does her bits and pieces.

What's her problem??? We've got *loads* of dobs on the upstairs landing! Brightens the place up, if you ask me.

So we get upstairs and go into the kitchen to make a cup of tea, and you'll never believe it, the kitchen cabinet's fallen off the wall again and half the cups and saucers are smashed.

Oh, and the telephone's been cut off. It turns out it's been cut off for days and we never even realised.

As Mum says, trying to look on the bright side, "It just goes to show how much we need it."

This is the story of my life. Tape no 2. To be continued…

Soon I'm going to have filled up another tape. That will be the third one! I can't believe I've found so much to say. I thought at first my life was completely empty, but now I see that quite a lot of things have been going on in it. It's only when you stop and think about it that you realise.

Something I haven't said anything about is when I was little. This is partly because I can't remember very much and partly because I think probably it would be quite boring. I don't want my book to be boring! This is the trouble with some of the books that Miss Foster reads to us at school. Right at the beginning they're a drag because you don't know what's happening or who the people are; and then just as you're starting to get into the story and thinking maybe this book is not so bad after all, you come to another draggy bit that makes you yawn and fidget and feel you never want to go near a book again *ever*, as long as you live.

I am trying very hard not to have draggy bits. That's why I've started my story when I'm old enough to talk and have opinions, and haven't bothered going back to babyhood. Babies are lovely but not very interesting in books, I don't think. What babies are best at is *doing* things.

crawling kicking

smiling playing crying cuddling

I expect I must have done all those things when I was a baby, but who wants to read about it? Not me!

So all I'm going to say is that I was born in the hospital and that for the first few years of my life we lived with Nan and Grandy in Soper Street, which is just round the corner from where we are now. I don't think Mum liked living with Nan. Nan used to nag her and tell her what to do and what not to do, like for instance whenever I cried she would tell

Mum "Not to go running! Let her get on with it."
But my mum is a big softie. She couldn't bear the
thought of me lying there crying so she didn't
take any notice of Nan. She used to cuddle me all
the time. I think this is right. When I have triplets
— two lots! — I will cuddle them. You bet!

Cuddling is what babies are for.

When I was about three, Nan and Grandy's
house was knocked down. The whole street was
knocked down and all the people, well, most of
the people, were sent to live on this new estate
way out at the end of the tube line. It's called
Arthur's Mill, because once upon a time, before
they went and built houses all over it, it was
owned by a man called Arthur who had a farm

and a windmill. It sounds lovely but in fact it is rather ugly and boring.

Nan likes it because she says it's a step up. From Soper Street, I suppose she means. She reckons it's dead superior, living on a new estate! But it is *grey* and *dreary* and it is UGLY. Not like Linden Close!

Anyway, Mum and Dad came to live in Bundy Street and that is where we have been ever since. And I have been at the same school, which is Spring Street Primary. And that is the story of my life up to the time I started writing this book!

Oh, I almost forgot: when I was five I had the chicken pox and got all covered in spots

some of which I *picked*.

Also there is a photograph of me with my front teeth missing.

Thank goodness I grew some new ones!

Chapter Six

I can't remember where I left off. I think it was the end of term, the day we broke up.

Yes, it was! I've just gone back and listened.

Everyone except me and Oliver had gone off to camp and I was stuck in London. Not that I'd have wanted to go to their rotten camp even if I could. Crammed in a barn with Tracey Bigg for two weeks? Ugh! No, thank you!

Just because it was school holidays didn't mean Mum could stay off work. She still had to go into Bunjy's and sell bread every day, like Dad still had to clean windows.

We discussed what to do about me, and I said that I'd be all right on my own. I don't mind being on my own! I quite like it, as a matter of fact. The one thing I begged Mum not to do was send me to my nan's.

I said, "*Please*, Mum! Please don't make me go away!"

I mean, partly it was 'cos I didn't want to leave Mum and Dad. I just didn't see how they would be able to manage without me. And partly it was 'cos I really really *hate* going to Nan's. I hate the way she picks on me and the way she grumbles all the time about Mum and Dad being rotten parents.

There was only one place I would have liked to go, and that was Croydon, to stay with Uncle Allan and Auntie Liz, but they wouldn't have me any more. I went there once and it was ever so lovely, only something really terrible happened: Auntie Liz sent me home in disgrace. I'd only been there a couple of weeks and she said she didn't want me in the house any more on account of my language. "Language of the gutter," she called it. She said, "We got out of London to avoid all that. I don't want my little Princess being contaminated."

Mum was really hurt and I felt ever so ashamed. *I* didn't know I spoke the language of the gutter. Dad just laughed. He said that Allan and Liz had become "proper toffee-nosed twits" since they'd moved to Croydon.

But when I stopped and thought about it I could see what Auntie Liz meant 'cos it's really

really nice in Linden Close, where they live. There's no mess or rubbish or burnt-out cars. There's no rude words sprayed on the walls. Nobody has punch-ups or gets drunk.

"Dead boring," says my dad. But I don't think it's boring! I think it's lovely. And I can understand why Auntie Liz doesn't want me to contaminate her little Princess.

The little Princess is my cousin Jade. I wish I had a beautiful name like Jade! It's a pity her surname is Small, as Jade Small doesn't sound very good, but maybe when she grows up she will marry a man called something grand such as Fairfax or Winstanley. These, I think, are very aristocratic.

Jade *will* marry someone aristocratic as she is extremely pretty, with dark curly hair and bright blue eyes. She is only four at the moment but already I can imagine how she will be when she is grown up.

I know it sounds truly yucky her mum and dad

Jade

Jade grown up

calling her their little Princess, but she is so beautiful that I can forgive them. Normally I wouldn't! Normally I would make vomiting noises.

But Jade is special, and everyone adores her.

I wish I hadn't upset Auntie Liz by using bad language! I mean, it was just, like, stuff we say all the time in the playground. The sort of stuff you don't even think about. But Auntie Liz moved to Croydon to get away from all that.

I wish she'd give me a second chance! But I don't think she will. Whenever she takes Jade to visit Nan and Grandy she always checks first that I'm not going to be there. She calls me "that child". I've heard her. I was at Nan's once and she rang up and I could hear her voice on the telephone. She said, "We'd like to come and see you next Sunday, Mum, but I wouldn't want to bring Jade if that child was going to be there."

Nan says she's quite right. She thinks I'm a real bad influence. Maybe when my book is published and I've made a lot of money and we can live in a nice house they will change their minds. I do hope so because I really love Jade! She is so funny and clever and sweet, and she's my only cousin in the whole wide world. I would be miserable if they never let me see her again.

But at the moment they don't want me anywhere near her in case I suddenly without thinking say something crude and vulgar, so Mum knew it wouldn't be any use asking if I could go to Croydon to stay. (Dad said he wouldn't let me in any case. "After they insulted us? No way! My Mand's worth a dozen of that little ponced-up miss." My dad always sticks up for me.)

I told Mum that I would be just fine on my own. I said, "I've been on my own before and I didn't burn the house down." Mum is more likely to burn the house down than I am!

Mum said, "Yes, but that was only for a few days."

See, it wasn't as if she just didn't bother. It wasn't like she just walked out and left me. She was really worried. She said, "You'll be here every day, all by yourself. What will you find to do all the time?"

I said that I would get on with my recording

for Cat, and do some wall painting, and clean the flat and do the shopping and the ironing and lay the table ready for Dad's tea.

"And on Saturdays we can have fun 'cos there won't be any work for you to do… I'll have done it all!"

Mum liked that idea. She got quite excited and started planning all the things we could do on Saturday afternoons as a family. She said, "We'll all go to places together. Think of some places where you'd like to go!"

So I made a list, which I have lost now, but these are some of the things that were on it:

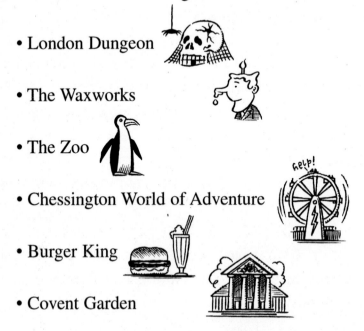

- London Dungeon

- The Waxworks

- The Zoo

- Chessington World of Adventure

- Burger King

- Covent Garden

I put Covent Garden because I once heard Tracey Bigg telling Aimee and Leanne that there was some street theatre there and it was fun. She'd seen people walking on stilts! I'd love to walk on stilts. I bet I could, too! I bet I'd be really good at it. I can already walk on my hands and do cartwheels.

Tracey Bigg can't. She tried in the playground and just went flump.

I was really looking forward to doing things as a family, and so was Mum. I don't expect, really, that we'd have been able to afford to do everything that was on my list, but we could have done *some* of them. We could have gone to Covent Garden to see the people on stilts, and we could have had a burger. And then maybe we'd have made a picnic and gone on the tube somewhere to eat it. Somewhere nice and green, like… like the park, or somewhere. We might even have looked at houses all day and chosen which one we'd like to buy when my book is published.

Whatever we would have done, it would have been fun. But the very first day of the holiday, it all went and got ruined.

I was really happy that day! I spent all morning doing wall painting, and then I opened a tin of tomato soup and put a packet of crisps in it (yum yum! Two of my favourites), and then I did a bit of recording, and then I thought perhaps I ought to do some housework, as I'd promised Mum, so I went and got the plastic sacks where she keeps the ironing and I was just setting up the ironing board when there's this ring at the door bell, which makes me jump, 'cos nobody ever rings at our door bell, hardly. And the ironing board goes and folds itself up on one of my fingers and makes me yell.

There's something wrong with the ironing board. Mum bought it second-hand at a boot sale and it's always collapsing. Dad's supposed to have looked at it, but he never has. Anyway, I don't expect he could do anything.

I went kind of slowly down the stairs, sucking at my finger 'cos it really hurt, and old Misery's peering out, all nosey parkering same as usual. She goes, "Who is it? Who are you expecting?" And then she tells me not to take the chain off 'cos it could be a mugger. She's always going on about muggers. She thinks there's a mugger hiding behind every dustbin.

Anyway, I kept the chain on, just to make her happy; I wasn't really expecting it to be a mugger. Afterwards I wished it had been. 'Cos what it was, it was even worse. It was my nan.

She said, "Oh, so you're here! I've been trying to ring you all week."

I explained that the telephone wasn't working, and she said, "You mean it's been cut off, I suppose," and made this cross tutting sound with her tongue. I said, "It wasn't their fault, they forgot to pay the bill. I should have reminded them. They have ever so many things to think about."

Nan said, "Rubbish! They're totally useless, the pair of them." And then she said, "Well! Aren't you going to let me in?"

So I let her in and we went upstairs and she said how she'd been going to ask old Misery Guts what had happened to us.

"I thought you'd all been murdered in your beds or your mother had finally managed to set fire to the place. Either that, or you'd been thrown out. Where is your mother, anyway?"

I said that Mum was at work and Nan nearly hit the roof.

"You mean she's left you here on your own?"

I said, "I'm old enough!" I wasn't going to have Nan slagging my mum off.

Nan said, "Don't be absurd, you're nowhere near old enough. A child of your age!"

I really resented that. I told Nan that in some countries there were people far younger than me out on the streets having to look after themselves. Nan said that didn't make it right and that Mum ought to be ashamed of herself. She said, "It's an absolute disgrace!"

I said, "Why pick on Mum?" It wasn't that I wanted to get my dad into trouble, but I didn't think it was fair, only having a go at Mum.

Nan said, "They're both as bad as each other. And where did you get that black eye?"

I didn't like to tell her I'd gone through the floorboard. She'd only have started on again about Mum and Dad being useless. I said, "I fell over in the playground." Nan made this snorting noise down her nose and said, "Fighting, I suppose."

Indignantly I told her that I didn't fight. "People pick on me."

"Oh, yes?" said Nan. "And what in heaven's name has been going on in here?"

She'd barged her way past me, into the kitchen. I have to admit, it did look a bit of a mess.

I started to explain that I hadn't yet got around to tidying up when there was yet another ring at the front door bell. I couldn't believe it! Twice in one day!

I said, "I'll go!" and went galloping back down the stairs.

Old Misery yelped, "You keep that chain on!" but this time I didn't 'cos I was just about sick of old Misery Guts and the way she kept poking her nose in where it wasn't wanted.

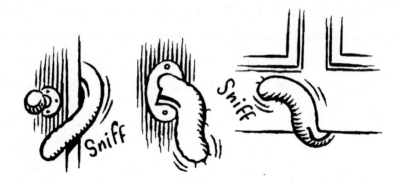

I thought that if it was a mugger I would ask him in and first he could mug Misery Guts and then he could go upstairs and mug my nan. I wouldn't let him mug me, I'd kung fu him!

But I reckoned he'd probably have done enough mugging by then. Anyway, it wasn't a mugger, it was Mum. She giggled and said, "Good thing you're here! I forgot my key." I said,  "Mum," trying to warn her, but she was in one of her bubbly moods and didn't listen. She set off up the stairs, burbling as she went.

"Eh, Mandy, guess what? Guess what old

Sourpuss gave me? A birthday cake! It was for this woman that never come to collect it, so she reckoned I might as well have it. It's got 'Happy Birthday Barny' on it, so I thought what we could do, we could change Barny into Barry and give it your dad and—"

That was when Mum reached the top of the stairs and bumped into Nan.

She said, "Oh! H–hello, Mum." Nan said, "Why has this child been left on her own all day? It's a disgrace!"

And then old Misery Guts' voice came shrieking up the stairs: "That's not the only thing that is!"

"What's she on about?" said Nan. She peered over the banisters and called down. "Who pulled your chain?"

"Ask them, ask them!" yelled Misery Guts. "Rowing and carrying on at all hours! They're not fit to have a child!"

"You just keep your lid on!" shouted Nan. "We don't need you shoving your oar in!"

"She's always having a go at us," said Mum.

"Yes, and not without cause, I'd say." Nan turned to go stomping back into the kitchen. "What's all this?" she said. She'd suddenly noticed the yellow blodges and the fried egg. I said it was paint, and Nan said she could see that, thank you very much.

"What's it doing there?"

So then I had to explain about the floorboard, and Mum told her about the water heater and how the landlord wouldn't do anything, and how the banisters had broken, and the kitchen cabinet wouldn't stay on the wall, and there were holes in the lino and the roof leaked and the whole place was just a tip; and Nan listened to it all with her face growing grimmer and grimmer.

"It's a death trap," said Mum.

"Yes," said Nan, "and you go waltzing off to work and leave this child to cope on her own."

"I can cope!" I said. "And Mum has to go to work 'cos we couldn't pay the bills otherwise."

"Don't you talk to me about paying bills!" snapped Nan; and I knew that I'd gone and said the wrong thing. "Look at this child!" said Nan. "Look at the state of her!"

"It was the floorboard," pleaded Mum.

"What was the floorboard?"

"How she got the black eye!"

"*Oh*?" Nan swung round on me. "What d'you want to go telling me lies for?"

"My Mandy doesn't tell lies!" cried Mum.

"I cannot believe—" Nan's bosoms sort of heaved upwards "— I cannot believe that it has come to this!"

"To w–what?" stammered Mum.

"*This*!" Nan flung out her arms. "I'm sorry, Sandra, but it cannot be allowed to go on. I am not having a grandchild of mine left all day and every day in this – this rubbish dump! That interfering old busybody downstairs is quite right. You're not fit to be parents. Either of you!"

"Mum and Dad can't help it," I said. "It's not their fault the house is falling to pieces, it's—"

"Amanda, will you please BE QUIET!" roared Nan.

My name isn't Amanda. It's Mandy.

"Just go to your room," said Nan. "I want a word in private with your mother."

She took Mum into the sitting-room and slammed the door, and I crept up and tried to listen but I couldn't hear very much, only the sound of Mum crying. And then the door opened and Mum came out and went running straight past me, all blotched and tear-stained, and Nan sailed after, looking like one of those things they have on churches that the water spouts out of.*

Really cross and horrible.

She said, "Right, that's settled. Go and get your bags packed. You're coming to live with me."

Not just stay with her.

Live with her.

It was my worst nightmare come true.

I don't really want to tell this next bit.

I'd rather tell something else.

Like, for instance... the day I went to my friend

*Note from Cat's mum: They're called gargoyles.

Janis's school sports and they had a PHAB race*
and Janis was in her wheel chair and I was
pushing her and we won first prize and had our
pictures in the paper.

That was great, that was! I'd much rather talk
about that than all about what happened next in
my life.

I mean, I don't *have* to talk about what
happened next. If I really don't want to. Nobody
can make me.

Except then perhaps they wouldn't publish it.
They would say, this girl is so boring, she is so
happy all the time with her mum and dad. Why
does nothing bad ever happen to her?

So I suppose I had better do it.

I suppose.

All right! I'll do it.

I shall take a **DEEP**
breath
and open my mouth
and just
talk.

*Query from Cat's mum: Does this stand for physically
handicapped-able-bodied? **Yes!**

Chapter Seven

When Nan said I was to go and live with her, my heart just fell right down with a great thunk! on to the floor. I knew it wasn't any use arguing. You can't argue with Nan. Once she's made up her mind, that's it.

But it was awful. It was really awful. Nan was all puckered and pursed, and Mum was just sobbing and sobbing, and then Dad comes home and says, "What's going on?" and Nan tells him what's happened, and how she's taking me away "Until you two get your act together", and Dad just goes mental. I mean, he just goes crashing and banging all about the place, and he's smashing his fist on things and shouting, and Misery Guts is howling up the stairs, and Mum's still sobbing, and Nan's trying to get Dad to calm down and "Listen to a bit of sense, for goodness' sake!" But Dad won't. Not for ages.

When at last he stops crashing and shouting,

he grabs me and pulls me to him and says, "You can't do this! You can't take my Mand!"

To which Nan retorts that if she doesn't take me it's only a matter of time before someone like old Misery Guts calls the Social Services.

"And once they get their hands on her, you can kiss her goodbye. She'll be sent to a children's home or put with foster parents, and that'll be that. And I wouldn't blame them, either! This way, I'm giving you a chance. You get yourselves sorted, I might consider letting you have her back. But I'm not having my grandchild brought up in a pigsty just because her mum and dad are too stupid and irresponsible to look after her properly. So there!"

There was a long silence after Nan said this. Dad went pale and even Mum stopped sobbing. Nan said, "Look at the place! Look at the state of it! You're like children, the pair of you. Just playing at keeping house. Look at this!" She ran a finger along the top of the mantelpiece. "*Filth*!"

I said, "I was going to see to that," but Nan turned on me, really sharp, and snapped, "It's not up to you!" And Dad chimed in with, "That's right.

It's not up to Mandy. It's up to her mum!" He glared at Mum as he said it, and that set Mum off crying again, and to my complete amazement Nan snarled, "Don't you try shifting all the blame on to Sandra! You're no better. Useless great lummock!"

I'd never known Nan turn on Dad before. It's always been Mum she's had a go at. But she was really mad. She kept on about "the Social" and how the shame of it would kill her. She said, "You'd just better pull your fingers out, the pair of you! Get this place cleaned up and start taking a few lessons in elementary house-keeping!"

Dad looked rebellious and started muttering, but Mum wept and said, "We will, we will!"

"Both of you," said Nan. "That means you, lummock!"

And she
actually poked
a finger right
in the middle
of Dad's chest.

Dad's jaw dropped way, way down.

I almost would have laughed, it looked so funny! But Mum was still sobbing, and there was my bag standing all packed and ready to go.

And any minute now Nan was going to say, "Right! That's it. Come along, Mandy," and I just couldn't bear it. I felt something hot and prickly happening in my eyes, and at first I couldn't imagine what it was but then it was like seeing everything through a window that rain is dripping down and I knew that I was crying.

But I don't cry! Not *ever*. I didn't even cry when the kitchen cabinet fell on me and cut my head open. Not even when I had to have stitches. Not even when Tracey Bigg makes up her horrid rhymes about me.

Crying is a sign of weakness. I didn't want to

cry! Nan said, "Come on, then, child. Let's get going," and I raced over to Mum and threw my arms around her and whispered, "I'll be back, Mum! Don't forget to make out shopping lists." If Mum doesn't make out shopping lists, she can't remember what she needs to buy. "And give Dad proper meals, Mum! 'Cos he needs them."

And then I raced over to Dad and hugged *him*, and begged him to be kind to Mum and not fly off the handle.

"Please, Dad! Don't get cross with Mum. I hate it when you do that!"

Next thing I know I'm being pushed down the stairs in front of Nan, and old Misery's there spying as usual, but for once she doesn't say anything, and we're out on the pavement and the front door's shut behind us and all I can think of is Mum sobbing and Dad going round bashing things.

Nan said, "It's the only way. They've got to learn. It's high time they grew up and started to behave like responsible adults."

But I loved my mum and dad just the way they were! I didn't want them to be any different. I hated Nan for taking me away from them. I felt that it was my fault. I felt like I'd let them down.

If only I'd tidied up the place before Nan had come! I could have made it look ever so nice. Really spick and span. Then maybe she wouldn't have got so mad. And I could have told her I wasn't really on my own, I could have told her old Misery was keeping an eye on me, or that I'd been over to Deirdre's, or just *anything*. Anything that would have stopped her having a go at Mum.

That first night when I said my special prayer, I added a bit at the end. After "For ever and ever" ten times, but before "Amen", I added, "And please let me go back to them soon. PLEASE!"

I just couldn't see how they were going to manage without me to keep an eye on them. I kept having these nightmares that Mum would do something daft and ruin Dad's tea and Dad would rise up in a rage and say that that was it, he'd had enough. And then he'd walk out and Mum would be on her own and she wouldn't know what to do, and she'd be so lonely, poor Mum! 'Cos we're the only people she's got in the whole world, me and Dad. And Dad would jump on a ship and go to Australia, which was what he was always threatening to do, and I wouldn't ever see him again.

I wasn't going to see them again for ages and ages, anyway. Nan had said she wanted them both to stay away until they had got themselves sorted. She said, "I want this girl given a fair chance. I don't want you coming round and upsetting her."

And Mum and Dad were ever so meek. They just did whatever Nan told them. She'd gone and scared them by saying how old Misery could go to the Social Services. Even Dad's scared of the Social Services, even if he does call them snooping do-gooders.

That first week at Nan's I said my prayer over and over, not just when I went to bed but when I woke up in the morning and lots of times in the day, as well. Once I was doing it, with my eyes screwed tight shut, when Nan started to say something to me. But I still went on doing it! Nan got angry and said why didn't I listen when she spoke to me? She said, "Are you sulking about something?"

I said, "No. I was thinking." Nan said, "Well, you just stop thinking and pay a bit of attention! It's very rude to go on thinking when someone's talking to you."

I could have told her it was rude to interrupt a person when they had their eyes closed, but you can't argue with Nan. She always likes to have the last word.

Grandy isn't so bad, but he is what Mum calls "under Nan's thumb".

He just likes to come home at tea-time and light his pipe and have a quiet life. During the day he is on guard in a bank, wearing a uniform and keeping an eye open for armed robbers. It is a great responsibility, guarding all that money, and I think Nan ought to let him rest when he comes in instead of keeping on at him the way she does.

What she mostly keeps on about is *me*. At least, that's what she kept on about while I was there. All about my manners and my language and how I hadn't got any decent clothes and look at my hair, it was just a mess, and "How am I supposed to take her anywhere?"

And Grandy just sat there and grunted, and puffed on his pipe, and you could tell he didn't really want to be bothered. Or maybe he didn't think I was quite as bad as Nan made out.

I thought at first I would never survive. I worried all the time about Mum and Dad and how they were managing without me and whether Mum was still crying and whether Dad was flying off the handle. And then at the weekend they telephoned me. I spoke to Mum first. She was still a bit tearful but she also giggled quite a lot as well.

She said, "Guess what? You'll never guess! We've gone back to school! Me and your dad… we're going to parenting lessons. Learning how to be good parents."

She said that Cat had called round, and when she'd heard what had happened she'd arranged for Mum and Dad to take these classes.

"They're ever so good," said Mum. "I'm really learning how to do things properly."

And then Dad came on and said, "How about

that, then? Your mum and dad doing lessons! We'll be different people, Mand, when you come home. You won't recognise us! We'll be model parents, we will."

I told this to Nan and she just sniffed and said, "That'll be the day." But then she added that any improvement had to be better than none.

After that, I began to feel a little less despairing and to believe that perhaps Nan really might let me go back home sometime. I still said my prayer with the special bit added, but now I only said it twice a day, once when I woke up and once before I went to sleep. I thought that if Mum and Dad were learning how to be model parents, perhaps I ought to make a bit of an effort to be a model granddaughter so Nan wouldn't be ashamed of me any more.

So I tried. I really, really tried! But Nan wasn't in the least bit grateful. Like, for instance, when we went shopping I said to her, "I'd better check your shopping list. Make sure you haven't forgotten anything." That's all I said, just trying to look after her, like I do with Mum. She nearly jumped down my throat!

She said, "What do you mean, *check my shopping list*, you bossy little madam? I'll check my own shopping list, thank you very much! I don't need your assistance. I haven't gone senile yet, you know."

Then another time I caught her doing sardines on toast for Grandy's tea. Sardines on toast! At the end of a hard day's work, guarding the bank! I knew I had to warn her. I said, "You really ought to give him a proper man's meal, Nan. They don't like just having bits of stuff on toast."

Whew! If I hadn't have had this really thick skin, her eyes would have bored through me like lasers. I'd have had all holes.

She said, "Are you presuming to tell me how to feed my own husband?"

She really didn't like me trying to help her, so after that I thought I'd help Grandy, instead. But even he didn't seem to appreciate it. Like one Saturday we went into town together and he was going to get some paint for doing the inside of the house and he actually bought *three different colours*. He got this goldy colour for the ceilings and green for the windows and white for making little lines round things. He said that Nan had chosen them.

"She likes the place to look nice."

I was horrified. I said, "But Grandy, it's ever so much more expensive using all those different colours! It's really wasteful. You ought to stick to just one. It works out far cheaper. And if you went down the market you might even find a bargain!"

That's what Dad did last year. He staggered home with simply gallons of paint that nobody wanted on account of it being a strange sort of orangey-browny colour. (A bit like sick, really.) So far he hadn't actually got around to using it, but he reckoned there was enough there to do the whole place with. And the colour wasn't actually too bad. I quite liked it, myself. I thought it was cheerful. Mum agreed. She said it was "eye-catching". But when I told Grandy about it he just chuckled and said, "Yes, I've heard about our Barry's orange paint. Your Nan would have a fit if I came home with something like that."

I said, "But think of the money you'd save!"

Grandy said, "Young lady, if your Nan wants her house painted three different colours, I think that's her business, don't you?"

You can't help people if they don't want to be helped. Another time when we went into town Grandy said he'd just got to nip in and place "a bob or two each way" on a horse. I don't know what a bob is, whether it's a lot of money or a little, but I remembered Dad going into the betting shop and spending all Mum's housekeeping money, and so I grabbed hold of Grandy's arm and said, "Grandy! No!"

Grandy looked at me in surprise. He said, "No what?" I said, "Don't go in there, Grandy! You'll only regret it! You'll spend all the housekeeping!"

Grandy didn't freeze me out like Nan had, but he did sound sort of... irritable. He said, "Good heavens, child! I've been having a little flutter once a month ever since I got married. I'm not going to stop now!"

It's odd that even though Nan and Grandy don't seem in the least bit worried about money, not really, I mean they don't fly into a panic when brown envelopes land on the mat and they've never once had their telephone cut off, they don't ever seem to *do* anything. They'll never suddenly jump up and say, "Let's have fun!" the way we do at home. They're like two stodgy dumplings, sitting in a stew.

One day when Nan was wondering what to give Grandy for his tea – "And kindly don't tell me that he needs a man's meal!" – I said, "P'raps we could go out  somewhere." Nan said, "Out? Out where?" I said, "Anywhere! We could go for an Indian meal."

Nan shuddered and said, "No, thank you! You won't catch me eating that muck." She said that she and Grandy didn't care for Indian food: "It doesn't agree with us."

So then I said, "Chinese?" and Nan said, "Chinese gives me a headache. Besides, you never know what they put in there."

"Burgers?" I said. But Nan said burgers weren't proper food and in any case, what did we want to go out for?

"It's a sheer waste of money. You can eat far better staying at home."

I said, "Yes, but it's not nearly as much fun!"

Nan just snorted and said, "There's more to life than just having fun. That's a lesson we all have to learn."

I didn't actually say it, 'cos I knew she'd tell me it was impertinence, but what I actually thought, inside my head, was, "I hope it's not what Mum and Dad are learning."

Mum and Dad and me always had fun. No matter what. Even if the house was falling down and we hadn't got any money and sometimes Mum cried and sometimes Dad yelled, we always, sooner or later, had a kiss and a cuddle and a bit of a laugh.

I think that is what life is all about.

This next chapter is going to be the very last one! It will be Chapter Number Eight, and I think that is enough for anybody. It must be extremely exhausting for Cat's mum, typing it all out.*

I'm glad Cat's pleased with it, though, 'cos I've worked really hard. *Really* hard. I mean, I've been sat here doing this tape every night, almost, when I could have been watching telly or wall painting or even reading a book. (Ha ha! That'll be the day.) But anything rather than just talk talk talk all the time. It wears you out, talking does.

I wish I could just do everything in pictures!

*Note from Cat's mum: Not at all! I'm quite enjoying it.

Chapter Eight

One day when I had been at Nan's for a fortnight, Grandy came home from work and said, "Guess what? There's a chum of yours staying just across the way."

I couldn't think what he was talking about. I don't have any chums. Not since my friend Janis got moved. I really miss Janis. We used to have ever such fun together.

Grandy said, "Someone who goes to your school," and my stomach fell plop! right down into my shoes.

"If it's Tracey Bigg," I said, "I hate her. She's my worst enemy."

Nan tutted and said, "Hate is a very extravagant word, my girl."

I said, "She deserves it. She's evil."

Nan opened her mouth to start on at me but Grandy got in first. He said, "Well, it's not Tracey Bigg, it's a boy called Oliver Pratt."

I said, "*Oliver*?"

"Now I suppose you'll tell us he's evil," said Nan.

"Oliver's all right," I said. "He's just a bit of a wimp."

"Well, he says you're his friend," said Grandy. "He's staying with his nan, same as you are, while his mum's at work."

It turned out that Oliver's nan lived in Soper Street, just up the road from Nan and Grandy. She'd been moved out to Arthur's Mill same time they had. But just 'cos our nans happened to live on the same horrible estate didn't make us friends!

"I said he could drop by," said Grandy. "Tomorrow morning, after breakfast. That all right?"

It didn't really matter whether it was or not. When grown ups go and arrange things for you, you're expected to just meekly do what they say and not make any sort of fuss. 'Cos if you *do* make a fuss, then heavens! You should hear them carry on.

So that's how I got lumbered with Oliver. Only actually, as it happened, it wasn't so bad.

I wasn't really looking forward to it. I mean, for one thing, Oliver reminded me of school, which is something I'd rather *not* have to think about during holiday time. For another, he's not exactly the brightest. Janis might have been in a wheelchair, but she was really smart. We had fun together! But poor old Oliver, he's – well! Not always quite with it.

So I woke up next morning thinking *"Oh, drear"* and gazing glumly into my cornflakes expecting the worst, and it just goes to show that sometimes things can turn out better than expected.

We spent that first day making up rhymes about Tracey Bigg. I told Oliver my one…

Tracey Bigg goes wah wah wah, When she talks it's all blah, blah!

and then he said that he'd got one, too. One that he'd made up all by himself.

Tracey Bigg Is a big fat pig.

I said, "That's great, Oliver! That's really ace."

You have to encourage him. It wouldn't have been kind to point out that a) his rhyme was an insult to pigs and b) not strictly speaking true, since Tracey Bigg is just BIG rather than fat.

Although I hate, loathe and utterly detest her, I think you should be honest about these things.

Here are some of the other rhymes we made up.

2, 4, 6, 8.
Who's the person
that we hate?
T.R.A.C.E.Y.

Oh dear, what
can the matter be?
Tracey Bigg is locked
in the lavatory!
She'll be there from
Monday to Saturday
And nobody jolly well
cares!

Actually, I sang a word that is ruder than "jolly" but I am thinking of Cat's mum and remembering that she doesn't like bad language and so I am trying to be polite.*

*Note from Cat's mum: Thank you! Very much appreciated!

Here is another one that Oliver made up.

Tracey Bigg's
a great fat cow.
I dont like her
anyhow!

This is another one.

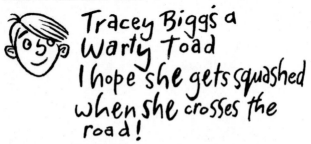

Tracey Biggs a
Warty Toad
I hope she gets squashed
when she crosses the
road!

He's got this thing about animals. He wanted to do one about her being a hippopotamus but he couldn't think of anything to rhyme with it.

This is one that I did.

Tracey Bigg is a total grot
Picks her nose and eats
her snot
Picks her scabs and chaws
them up
Makes you feel like
throwing up.

BLUUUUUURGHGH!

She does pick her nose and eat it. I've seen her doing it. She's disgusting!

Someone once told me that if you keep picking your nose, your head will cave in.

Ha! That would be something.

Next day I went round to Oliver's place. Well, Oliver's nan's. He'd got something he wanted to show me. It was this bit of garden his nan had given him. Just this little patch right at the end. He'd had it since he was eight years old, and it was all full of flowers, just like my bedroom wall except that these were *real* – and it was Oliver who'd planted them!

What was totally and utterly amazing was that he knew all their names. I'd say, "What's this pink one?" and he'd say, "That's an anemone." And then I'd say, "What's the blue one?" and he'd say, "That's a delphinium."

He probably couldn't spell them (neither can I!) but he knew all there is to know about them, like what sort of soil they grow in and when you have to plant them and whether they're the kind that come up every year or the kind that die out.

Being really interested in flowers myself, because of the garden that I am one day going to have, I learnt as much as I could and tried to store it all inside my head. What I did was I drew pictures of all the flowers that Oliver had grown and put their names by them.

I bet Tracey Bigg doesn't know half as much as Oliver! I bet she doesn't know *any*thing. I think  Oliver's really clever, being able to grow all those flowers and remember their names. Nobody helped him. He did it all on his own. I thought to myself that I would tell Cat about Oliver's flower garden when we went back to school. She'd be dead impressed! It's almost as good as writing a book.

Maybe *as* good. In a different way.

Oliver was only staying with his nan for three weeks. After that, he and his mum and dad were off to Ireland to live in a caravan for a bit. I would love to stay in a caravan! I think it would be really neat.

You would have little beds one on top of the other, and little tables that folded away when you didn't want to use them, and a little stove for cooking on, and a little teeny bathroom with a shower.

Everything would be lovely and warm and cosy and if you met someone you didn't like, such as for example Tracey Bigg, you would simply drive on to somewhere else.

Oliver said that the caravan he and his mum and dad stay in in Ireland isn't the sort that you could drive places in. It is in a caravan park and cemented to the ground.

I don't care. It would still be fun!

I felt a bit miserable when Oliver went off to Ireland. I suppose I'd sort of got used to having him around. He promised he'd send me a postcard with an Irish stamp on it, and he did! It's lovely. On the front there's this picture of a little funny creature that Nan said was called a leprechaun

and on the back he'd written a message:

Dear Mandy
    How are you?
        Love Oliver.

It wasn't much of a message, I suppose, but it gave me a happy feeling, especially as nobody had ever sent me a postcard before. Also I know that it is very difficult for Oliver to pick up a pen and write real words. I expect his mum and dad had to help him. He is a worse speller even than me!

He is also funny – he makes me laugh when he does his Tracey Bigg rhymes! – but a bit pathetic, as well, so from now on I am going to look after him. We have vowed that we will stay together, and when Tracey Bigg or the Murdo gang start their nonsense I will stick up for us. Oliver has said that he will stick up for us, as well, but I don't think it would be wise to rely on him. But that is all right! I can do it for both of us.

I won't mind so much about going back to school now that Oliver and me have decided to be friends. It's not so bad if you have someone to go round with. You can share things and have secrets and tell each other jokes. And we can sit together in class and choose each other for partners. And it won't matter if people jeer and sneer and say we're no-hopers, 'cos there'll be two of us.

Anyway, we're not! Oliver has his flower bed, and I have written a book!

Well, nearly. When I've finished this chapter I will have.

Once a week while I was at Nan's, Mum and Dad rang me to report how they were getting on at their classes. They were ever so excited about it! Mum said, "We're coming along a treat, Mandy! The teacher said that being willing to learn is half the battle."

Dad said, "We'll be reformed characters. You'll see!"

Nan still wouldn't let them come and visit me. She said that they had got to learn how to stand on their own two feet, and that it would only unsettle me. She said, "You're doing very nicely. I don't want them coming and setting you back again."

Wow! It was news to me that I was doing very nicely. I'd thought I was just one big pain in the you-know-what.

Then one day Auntie Liz rang up and I listened at the door while Nan was speaking to her.

I know you're not supposed to eavesdrop but I wanted to hear if Nan talked about me, which she did, so I reckon that made it OK. If people are going to talk about you then I think it's only fair you should be able to listen to what they're saying. That's what I think.

Anyway, this is what I heard Nan say. She said, "As a matter of fact, her manners have improved by leaps and bounds since she's been with us. She's quite a different child, you'd hardly know her."

me!

Next Auntie Liz said something that I couldn't hear, and then Nan said, "I don't think you'd need have any worries. She's not a bad girl at heart. I'm really quite proud of her."

Help! Faint!

That weekend, Uncle Allan and Auntie Liz came to visit, and they brought Jade with them. Jade remembered me! She was ever so happy to see me, she cried, "Mandy, Mandy!" and came running over for a cuddle. I remembered my manners and talked dead posh, just like the Queen and was as good as good can be. They let me take

Jade into the garden and we played skipping games and hopping games and I didn't use gutter language once!

When they went home that evening Auntie Liz said, "Well, Mandy! We'll have to see about getting you down to visit us some time."

I never *ever* thought she'd let me go to Croydon again. It didn't exactly make up for being away from Mum and Dad, but it did give me this lovely warm feeling of being approved of.

Yah boo and sucks to Tracey Bigg! I bet she hasn't got a little cousin like Jade.

I was so grateful to Nan for telling Auntie Liz nice things about me that I thought I really ought to start making more of an effort to be helpful to her, and I racked my brains thinking what I could do. She wouldn't let me check her shopping lists or make suggestions about what to give Grandy for his tea. But there had to be something!

And then I had an idea and thought that as a surprise I would re-organise her kitchen for her while she was upstairs one day having her afternoon nap. I did this for Mum, once, and she was ever so pleased. She said, "Oh, Mandy, that's brilliant!" It was, too. Before I got at it Mum's kitchen had been a proper mess, what with saucepans on the floor and the chip pan under the cooker (once we even found *mouse droppings* in it).

Nan didn't have saucepans on the floor and she didn't have a chip pan at all, 'cos she uses oven-ready, but I could think of all kinds of things I could do that would be an improvement.

First I moved the vegetable rack and put it

where the saucepans were, then I put the saucepans where the waste bin was, and then I put the waste bin by the back door.

Next I re-arranged all the cups on their little hooks, and then I changed the plates and cereal bowls around, and then I put the spice rack over near the cooker and tidied up all the sieves and the ladles and the things for crushing garlic and for chopping eggs and mashing spuds. Nan has a whole load of stuff in her kitchen! Ever so much more than Mum.

It took me a whole hour to get it all worked out. It looked really good! I honestly thought Nan would be pleased with me.

But she wasn't.

She made me put it all back again.

"*Everything…* just the way you found it!"

I said, "But, Nan, it didn't make sense the way you'd got some of this stuff. I mean, you need *saucepans* by the *cooker*. And the *waste* bin—"

Nan said, "I'll have my saucepans where I've always had my saucepans, if you don't mind! *And* my waste bin."

I tried ever so hard to be patient with her. Because, I mean, she is quite old. I explained how she really needed to plan things so she didn't have to keep walking to and fro all the time. I said, "You see, Nan, it's a terrible waste of energy. When people get to your age—"

Nan just exploded. There was, like, steam coming out of her ears.

She said, "Mandy Small, I have had just about as much as I can take of you and your bossy ways! I think it's high time you went back and bossed your mum and dad, instead."

Oh! I was so happy I rushed right across the kitchen and hugged her.

Me! Hugging Nan! I've never done such a thing in my life before. Nan just isn't a hugging sort of person.

But she didn't seem to mind. She said, "I reckon you'll do. Though whether those parents of yours will have learnt anything is another matter."

I didn't care whether Mum and Dad had learnt anything or not. I just wanted to get back to them!

The day I came home was the VERY BEST DAY OF MY LIFE. Mum threw her arms round

me and I threw my arms round Mum and Dad
threw his arms round both of us and we laughed
and cried until we couldn't
laugh or cry any
more.

Mum and Dad
wanted to tell
me all about
their classes
they'd been
having.

"We've
learnt a thing
or two, Mand!"

"We're going to be model parents from now on!"

Then Dad wanted to show me all the things
he'd done around the place while I'd been away.

"See? I've put up that shelf in your bedroom at
long last."

He had, too! He'd chopped up Nan's horrible
old wardrobe and now I had the shelf that I'd
always wanted. (I didn't ask where my clothes
were going to go 'cos that might have upset them.
At the moment they were all in piles on the floor,
but I thought probably we'd be able to find a rail
or something at a boot sale. Anyway, who cares

about clothes! My shelf was more important.)

Mum said that she'd been round the second-hand shops finding little ornaments to go on it.

"Little cats and dogs... I knew you'd like those."

As well as Dad doing things the Council had got on to the landlord and now we had a brand new water heater that worked first time without blowing the place up.

The floorboards had been fixed, and so had the roof.

And Dad had used up all his orangey-browny paint! He'd painted everything – the landing, the kitchen, the sitting-room, his and mum's bedroom, my bedroom, even the ceilings. They were all orangey-browny!

"Doesn't it look beautiful?" said Mum.

It did! It looked beautiful. Not really like sick at all.

"See, we've turned over a new leaf," said Mum. "We're going to keep the place nice from now on."

"That's right," said Dad. "Keep it in good nick."

"No more black eyes. No more broken heads."

"No more accidents of any kind. Come and have a look at this!"

Dad grabbed me by the hand and whizzed me into the kitchen. "See that?" He pointed, ever so proudly, at the kitchen cabinet. It was back on the wall. "There for good, this time," said Dad. "That won't be coming down again in a hurry!"

After I'd been shown all the wonderful things that had happened while I was away, Mum suddenly said, "Oh, I almost forgot! Miss Daley called about an hour ago. There's something she wants to tell you. She said it was important. You'd better ring her."

Me, ring Cat?

"I haven't got her number," I said.

"I have," said Mum. She sounded really pleased with herself. "Look! I wrote it down. See?"

"Does she really want me to ring her?" I said. I don't know why, but for some reason I suddenly felt nervous. I mean… *me*? Ring Cat?

"Yes, go on!" said Mum. "I'll dial it for you."

I just couldn't believe it when Cat told me the news. She said that "some bits of my book" – what she called "extracts" – were going to be put on display at the Town Hall! She said it was an exhibition of "creative activity" in the borough and that I'd been chosen out of hundreds of others.* What we had to do was get together and decide which bits we wanted to use. Not, *unfortunately*, the bits about Tracey Bigg! Cat said, "Some of the bits with the drawings. How about that?"

Fine by me! The drawings are what I like best. So now, yippee, I'm a Real Author!

"Of course, you do realise," said Cat, and she sounded sort of anxious, "there won't be any money attached to it?"

I knew that! I've known all along that I wouldn't really make my fortune. That was just a game I played. Pretending. I was just happy that everyone was going to see my name!

Mum and Dad were really thrilled.

"Get that!" chuckled Dad. "Our Mand's going to be a celebrity!"

"Yes," I said, "and I've drawn pictures of you and Mum, so you'll be celebrities as well. And I won't give any secrets away," I added, just in case he was still bothered.

*Note from Cat's mum: Well done!

But Dad was too proud and excited to care about secrets.

"This calls for a celebration!" he cried; and he decided that we would all go up the road to the Indian restaurant.

So that was what we did. And it was a really perfect evening. It started off being happy and it ended up even happier. Mum didn't cry, and nothing got spilt, and as we walked home Dad sang some of his Elvis songs while me and Mum swung hands.

I love my mum and dad! They'd tried so hard while I'd been away. They'd done so much. But I couldn't help giving this little secret smile as I looked at that kitchen cabinet. I thought to myself, "I bet it won't still be up there this time next week…"

Guess what? *Kerrash!!!*

I was right. It wasn't!

Fruit and nut case, here I come!

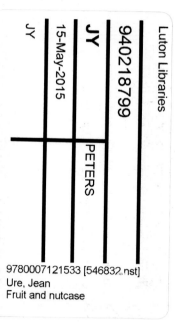

Printed by RR Donnelley at Glasgow, UK